Fractured Allegiance

by Allen Manning & Brian Manning
Cover by Allen Manning

Copyright © 2018 Allen Manning

All rights reserved.

CHAPTER
1

The helicopter's rotors thrummed, slicing through the air and buffeting Lieutenant Curtis Clarke with the choppy wind. A rapid drum beat thumped his chest, rattling the gear on his rig. He had one foot already out of the side of the Blackhawk, eyes squinted, watching as the pilot brought his team closer to the landing zone.

He and his men were in pursuit of a group of mercenaries operating within the US border illegally. They had already taken one team into custody with minimal conflict, and Curtis hoped to do the same today.

"Let's do this clean and by the numbers," he said over his mic as the helicopter reached its destination.

A pair of ropes dropped out, one on either side of the hovering craft to the ground below. Curtis and his men slid down, immediately drawing their weapons and covering the rest of the team as they descended onto the road leading up the bridge. A police roadblock closed off the far end, but a loose police presence on this side allowed the few cars and people to flee, getting them out of a potentially dangerous situation

At three o'clock in the morning, traffic was sparse, only a few cars were left behind near a matte black H2 Hummer parked three-quarters of the way down. The police had successfully evacuated all of the innocent bystanders, but a several had to leave their cars behind, unable to turn them around to get away.

With his full team on the deck and ready to go, Curtis gave the order to move ahead. With practiced precision, each man held an M4 carbine pressed into his shoulder, elbows tucked. They looked down their weapon's sight as they walked along the bridge, taking smooth steps to maintain their aim on the target vehicle.

"Don't take your eyes off of the truck," Curtis said.

"Two tangos exiting on the far side," Jimenez said.

Curtis signaled for his team to take cover. Bracing their weapons on the empty vehicles, they kept their aim on the Hummer and waited. One of the mercenaries raised his hands, holding a rifle over his head by the stock and foregrip, hand away from the trigger.

"We give up. Don't shoot."

Curtis narrowed his eyes, and his throat tightened. "Step out with your hands up."

The two men obeyed his orders, one still holding his weapon up, the other letting an AR-15 hang from its sling.

Curtis stepped out, followed by two of his men. The other two held their positions, guarding the vehicle.

"There's still two inside," the one holding the rifle said.

"Tell your buddies to hang it up," Curtis said. "It's over."

The man with the hanging rifle shifted his gaze quickly between Curtis and the driver.

The hairs on Lieutenant Clarke's neck stood on end, and his gut screamed something was off.

"Look out!" one of his teammates shouted.

A burst from inside the truck shattered the driver side window, and an AK-47 unleashed a hail of bullets at the HRD team. The mercenary with the rifle hanging from a sling ran to the far side of the Hummer and brought his weapon up.

Before the man could fire, Curtis dropped to a knee and put the glowing red dot of his targeting reticle on the man's chest. He gave the trigger a pair of smooth presses, and the M4 bucked. Two wet thwacks sounded, as neat little holes appeared side by side on the man's chest before he fell from view. Higher pitched bursts shook the air, as his men returned fire on the driver, killing him.

Without wasting any more time, Curtis seized the momentary lapse in their enemy's bravery and ordered his team to move forward. All five HRD operatives stepped with a smooth pace, weapons held steady from hours upon hours of intense training.

As the dust settled, they could hear the man in the back seat shouting from inside the vehicle. He had one hand pressed on the window and the other waving out from the shattered driver side door showing he was unarmed. The other mercenary outside of the vehicle tossed his weapon down when the fighting started and was now curled on his side, eyes bugging out.

"We surrender, please don't kill us." His voice cracked and trembled.

Curtis yanked the back door open, keeping his weapon braced against his shoulder, and the team swarmed the vehicle. Two men hauled the suspect out, flattening him, stomach down on the asphalt. The other two team members pulled the last man around, also forcing him down and securing his hands behind his back.

Curtis circled around the vehicle slowly. He saw the man he shot, lying dead on the surface with a pair of bloody holes grouped close together to the left of his sternum. He used the toe of his boot to work the weapon sling around the dead man's shoulder and kicked the rifle away. Curtis continued his search, making sure no more hidden surprises were waiting for his team.

"All clear," he said.

"Clear," each of his men responded in turn.

"Signal the go ahead. Law enforcement can clean up this mess, now." Curtis said. He keyed his mic. "Dr. Spencer, get the truck in here so we can secure these two."

"Roger that, Lieutenant Clarke."

"I think this is the last of them, Stone," Curtis said.

"I believe you're right," John replied. *"Great job, Lieutenant. First round's on me."*

Fractured Allegiance

The Manning Brothers

CHAPTER
2

Marvin Van Pierce, Director of the Hostile Response Division, walked into the room. The team was already inside, and those who weren't already standing rose to their feet when the Director entered. Parker Lewis, the computer specialist, still sat in his seat, oblivious, his eyes fixed on the screen of his laptop. John Stone nudged Parker's chair with a stiff knee.

"Oh, yeah, sorry about that, sir," he said staggering to his feet and easing his computer closed.

"Relax everyone," Van Pierce said, placing a folder at the head of the table before sitting down.

The rest of the team took their seats. Except for Parker, who looked around, confused. "I just stood—never mind," he said sitting next to John.

Director Van Pierce eyed Parker, almost letting a smile show on his face. "Are we finished, Mr. Lewis?"

Parker just nodded, pressing his lips together.

"First, I want to say congratulations. With yesterday's operation, we've successfully eliminated the remaining mercenary companies operating on U.S. soil." Marvin opened the folder and glanced down at the top sheet. "We will question them all, and find out definitively, but it's believed they were all acting in connection with the recently deceased Warren Ratcliffe."

"Or at least the man that passed his orders down to Ratcliffe," Dr. Miranda Spencer added. She adjusted her glasses, looking at a copy of the report the HRD director also had.

"Do we know who that may be yet?" John asked. "The man above Ratcliffe, I mean."

"Not at this time," the director said. "With the amount of data you and Parker were able to bring to us, I have no doubt that information will be discovered, but it's going to take time."

"You dropped a mountain of files on us," Curtis Clarke said with a smirk. "The analysts are going to be pulling double shifts to rake through all of that."

"I have a question, sir," Parker said, raising a hand.

"Put your hand down, son. Just ask your question, this isn't elementary school," Marvin said.

"Ok, uh, I know we haven't heard back from the teams handling the interrogations, but do the analysts have an idea what the contractors were doing?" Parker folded his hands on the table. "They weren't targeting anyone, and they weren't taking anything from the locations they hit."

"Initial reports suggest a high probability that they were intelligence operations," Van Pierce said.

"Most likely the man calling the shots covering his tracks," John said. "None of these companies had any involvement until after Ratcliffe's death."

"We just need to keep doing what we're doing until the data comes back, and we get a clearer picture," the director added.

* * *

After the meeting, John jogged down the hall to catch up to Director Van Pierce. "Sir, may I have a word?"

Marvin stopped and turned. "Of course, Stone. What is it?" He started walking down the hall again as John fell into step at his side.

"I just think we should be focusing much more on the shot caller. The man that handed the orders down to Ratcliffe."

"How do you know it's a man?" Marvin asked with a smirk. "I understand, but are you sure this isn't just your desire to seek vengeance for a friend?"

John stopped and faced Van Pierce. "I'd be lying if I said that wasn't a part of this, but you and I both know this is much bigger."

Marvin stopped and put his hands in his pockets. "Yes, it is. That's why we need to be careful about how we approach the next few steps."

"We've seen what these guys are capable of," John said. "If this mystery man at the top is sending merc units to destroy evidence, he's not on the run or going into hiding. He intends to stay right where he his."

"And while he's doing that, we'll keep getting closer to revealing his identity," Marvin said. "I appreciate your drive, but this is a massive threat we're taking on. One mistake, one wrong move, and we lose the advantage."

"Are you sure we've got the advantage?" John asked. "I'm only asking for a bit of leeway to start looking for a name. Something that's possibly not in the files we've already got."

The director smiled. "Just you? Strap on your kit, grab your gun and start roughing people up until they spill the beans?"

John stood up straighter, holding his hands behind his back. "I would need some support. Parker."

"I'm starting to sound like a broken record, but you're in no condition to be doing field work. You had a building fall on top of your head not even a month ago."

"I've been sidelined for the past three and a half weeks, sir. Not even training." John paused for a moment and relaxed his posture. "I'm not some hot shot out looking for a fight. I'm talking strictly gathering information."

Marvin put a hand on John's shoulder. "John, I know what you're asking, but I need you to trust the team. They know what they're doing, and our analysts will be putting all of the information together as fast as they can. Reports will be generated hourly, so if anything comes up, we'll know.

"You and Curtis have worked together quite well these past few weeks," Marvin said. "Your presence in the operations center has been invaluable. I just need you to continue in that role until we've got something actionable."

"Clarke's a natural leader," John said. He folded his arms and shifted his weight back. "I can do that, sir."

"Thank you." Director Van Pierce turned on his heels and continued down the hall.

John stood in place for another moment, listening to the *click clack* of the director's dress shoes as the receded into the distance. He knew Van Pierce was right. The team worked well together, and they accomplished a lot in a short amount of time.

CHAPTER
3

Pryce Windham cut an imposing figure. Standing at over six feet tall, tipping the scales at just under two hundred pounds, he followed a strict workout regimen to maintain his physique. His spacious office was sparsely decorated, with a minimum amount of clutter. He sat at a thick, tempered glass and brushed steel desk, kept clean with no useless papers or office supplies.

The dark stained oak walls complemented the black and gold marble floors, making the already spacious office feel even more vast. Pryce leaned back in his chair, with his new enforcer, Mr. Gordon, standing at his side.

A man addressed Pryce, clutching his hands in front of his stomach and occasionally wiping away sweat from his brow or upper lip with a trembling finger. Outside of Windham's office, this man, in charge of a powerful private security company, would command great respect, and in some cases fear. But here, now, in front of Pryce Windham, Ruben Shields was a near quivering bundle of nerves.

"I'm sorry, Mr. Windham, I just—"

Pryce waved his hand to silence the man. He stood and smoothed a hand back over his silver hair before straightening his tie.

"What were your objectives, Ruben?" Pryce planted both fists on his desk, leaning forward as he spoke.

"I, I mean, my men were to destroy all compromising information." Ruben rolled a shoulder and tugged at his collar with a finger. "And retrieve, if possible—"

"No," Pryce said. "Your only orders were to inflict sufficient damage to the data systems to make retrieval of the information impossible. Not to retrieve. Not to copy. Destroy."

"I just thought that—"

"I don't pay you to think. I pay you to act."

Mr. Gordon straightened his posture and unbuttoned his jacket as Pryce's voice shook the room. Ruben stammered and took a step back.

"Mr. Windham, we got word that you needed to backup all data in a central location," the man stammered.

"It's two thousand eighteen, Mr. Shields." Pryce crossed his arms over his chest. "Did you think that our facilities aren't networked to make passing data back and forth, a simple matter?"

Ruben opened his mouth to say something, then thought better of it. His lips clamped shut with an audible pop.

"We are able to move said data from one point to another as easily as Mr. Gordon crossing this room to reach you."

The lithe, silent killer walked across the marble floor, stalking the defense contractor. Mr. Gordon stopped right in front of Ruben and clasped his hands behind his back. The stance was non-threatening, but his jacket opened far enough to reveal a handgun holstered to the right of the enforcer's belt buckle.

"Your men had simple orders, Shields. Connect and detonate the EMP charges, and burn any hard copies. Nothing about pulling data, or leaving the premises with any of it."

Ruben swallowed, still talking to Pryce as his eyes remained glued to the Glock 21 Mr. Gordon carried. "My mistake, sir. I—I promise to rectify the issue."

"And what issue is that?" Pryce asked, sitting down again. "This, Hostile Response Division that secured the drives your men had in their vehicle when they were apprehended."

The imposing man sat and rested his elbows on the desk with one hand inside the other, pressing them to his chin. His enforcer circled behind Ruben with slow, measured steps. Ruben tried to speak, but Pryce held up a hand to stop him.

"Yours was a huge mistake. The kind of mistake that gets people killed."

"Please, Mr. Windham, let me fix this." The man pleaded.

A hand clamped down on Ruben's shoulder, causing him to flinch and tense up. The silence stretched for seconds, and Mr. Gordon released his grip. Ruben recoiled again, waiting for terrible things to happen.

"Your performance over the past couple of weeks may be enough to overlook this, however," Pryce turned to retrieve a small stack of papers from a file cabinet behind him. "Of the three teams we used, your men accomplished the majority of the dozen or so such jobs we required. And for that, I'm going to let you leave my office of your own accord."

"Thank you, Mr. Windham. Thank you," Ruben said, voice warbling. He backed away, nearly bumping into Mr. Gordon, but the enforcer stepped to one side smoothly, allowing the man to kowtow his way out of the office. "You can count on me to make this right."

"We'll be in touch," Pryce said, as Ruben closed the door behind him.

"You should have let me kill him," the enforcer said.

He faced Mr. Gordon again. A half smile pulled at one corner of his mouth. Pryce was looking at a man that, just weeks ago, suffered a broken back at the hands of John Stone. It was the type of devastating injury that left many men and women unable to walk for life.

Windham's organization spent a fortune on research and development, focusing much of it on military applications. Several of the programs were devoted to making soldiers more combat effective. It was from those programs that they designed the implants used throughout Mr. Gordon's body, running along his back, which restored his fighting effectiveness.

The enforcer's spinal column would never heal, but the experimental technology helped the signals bridge that gap. Combining the surgical procedure with cutting-edge treatments and therapy also granted his enforcer vastly increased physical attributes. Mr. Gordon was now stronger, faster, and much more deadly than before.

CHAPTER

4

"We're just borrowing the data," Parker said. "Not even the actual data, just a copy of it."

"I understand how computers work, Parker. But it's not worth ruffling any feathers," John said.

"I bet more than a few of these people on here are up to something. Like this dude, Kevin Dalling," Parker said, jabbing a finger at the list of names from one of his surface-level searches. "That name sounds nefarious."

"Just sounds like a regular name to me," John said.

"You said it yourself, you told Van Pierce that we should be out digging up more information. Climb up the ladder, find how who's really in charge."

"And now I agree with Director Van Pierce. There's a team of analysts poring over the intel, and they've got the same goal in mind."

Parker scoffed, pretending to be offended. "You think those bachelor's degrees in the geek squad can find something?"

"Yes," John said, propping his hands on a desk and leaning back.

"Well, yeah, I guess. There's more of them, and their computers probably cost more than mine."

"Probably?"

"Hey, you don't know how much cash I've dumped into this rig," Parker said, pointing to his laptop.

John smiled. "Let's just play this the HRD's way."

"I should at least be in there helping out," Parker said, stuffing his laptop into a messenger bag.

John headed for the door. "When the team has more information, we can revisit this conversation."

"And if we don't have enough info?" Parker asked.

"They'll send Curtis and his team out to run the ops necessary to gather some more."

"Lieutenant Clarke? What's he gonna do, shoot at the computers until they spit out the info he's looking for?"

"What do you have against Clarke?" John asked.

Parker's shoulders sagged. He picked up his bag and looped the strap over his head. "Nothing. I'm just feeling a little useless here."

"You had a pretty exciting month, kid. What's wrong with just relaxing for a couple of weeks, enjoying all this fresh, bullet-free air?"

Parker chuckled, scratching his chest under the strap of his bag. "Point taken. But if MVP doesn't deliver in two weeks, I'm *borrowing* a few gigs of data and seeing what I can find."

John just shook his head, unable to hide his smile. "Good night, Parker." The big man headed down the hall and turned a corner.

"Yeah," Parker said, puffing his chest out. "Yeah."

CHAPTER 5

Mr. Gordon flexed his arms, opening and closing his hands. Since the treatments that rebuilt his body, it was a subconscious act. Before he came face to face with John Stone, he was serious about his physical conditioning. After suffering paralysis at the hands of his foe, Mr. Gordon emerged a different man altogether. A machine. A product of science and technology. Though still flesh and blood, the muscles running along his denser skeletal structure were like braided steel cables, dense and compact.

He was given explicit instruction about the package as it was handed to him by Pryce Windham himself. The small, padded envelope had no external information or discernable markings. Mr. Gordon memorized the delivery address before slipping it into the inside pocket of his kevlar motorcycle jacket.

"This goes to the Senator, personally," Pryce had said. "No aides, no couriers, no middlemen. From your hand to hers."

The enforcer understood the gravity of the job he had been given. He didn't know the contents of the envelope, and he didn't care. He had no ambitions for control and power himself.

Born and bred to be a warrior, he reveled in besting any opponent that stepped in his path. Mr. Gordon had never known defeat until he faced John Stone. The tingling pulses he felt from the implants along his spine were a permanent reminder of that bitter night.

He stood before his Ducati Diavel, his fists clenched tight. He forced his mind to relax and reminded himself of the job at hand.

You'll meet that man again, and next time the outcome will be much different, he thought, before slipping a helmet over his head.

Draping a leg over the Ducati's seat and started it up. The bike's 150 plus horsepower engine roared to life. Mr. Gordon pulled onto the busy street, opening the throttle up as he flew past the traffic.

***

Pryce circled around and sat at his desk. Since the death, and resulting investigation, of Warren Ratcliffe by the government's Hostile Response Division, he had to move fast to distance himself and his associates from the man.

The attempts made to pull all incriminating information to a central location failed when Ruben Shields' team had not only been taken in alive but also in possession of a portable hard drive containing sensitive materials. Now, time was no longer on Windham's side. He had to regain control of the situation no matter the cost.

The next steps of his plan would require an enormous expenditure of his political capital, accrued at no small expense, over years of quid pro quo maneuvering, and the collection of information that would help, or hurt, careers in Washington D.C.

Pryce reread the report in front of him, detailing the plan for the government to exert more control over the Hostile Response Division. The team, run by Marvin Van Pierce, would now be falling under the control of principal officials answering to Pryce Windham, albeit indirectly.

His eyes fell to the notes, moving over the same few lines over and over. The report mentioned the confrontation with John Stone, flagging him as a potential problem. A suggestion was included to place

Stone in a limited role, with on-base supervision, to ensure his compliance.

John Stone was the man directly responsible for killing Warren Ratcliffe, and destroying the PEST prototype, as well as preventing Windham's acquisition of Project: Guardian. If nothing were done about this maverick, Stone would quickly become a problem that would be too much for his assets to handle.

Pryce thumbed through the recent calls on his phone and found the name he was looking for. After two rings, a voice on the other end answered.

"I received your report," Pryce said.

"Yes, it's satisfactory, covering everything I need to know. I'm giving you full approval to proceed, but you'll need to amend the stated objectives first."

"What do you need?"

"It's John Stone. Your assertion was correct, he will be an issue if left unchecked, but I find your suggested course of action insufficient."

Pryce turned in his chair looking out the window. "Left unchecked, a rabid dog can be quite troublesome. He needs to be put down."

He listened thoughtfully, then responded.

"No, we do it through the proper channels. Publicly. Make sure the name John Stone is synonymous with domestic terror."

CHAPTER
6

Director Van Pierce scrolled the map on the projected display, focusing on the eastern coast of the United States. Curtis Clarke and John Stone stood in the command room with him.

"It looks like we've got several points of interest further north, in upstate New York." Van Pierce said.

"That's where the data facility exploded not too long ago, right?" Curtis asked.

"Yes, and it appears that at least one of these other locations may be tied to that particular facility."

"Who hit the other site?" John asked. "Our guys?"

"We still don't know," the director answered. "All reports from government and law enforcement cite *faulty utilities*."

"They're giving us that tired *gas leak* explanation?"

Van Pierce smiled. "Seems that way, but if there's another player involved, we need to find out ASAP."

"Yes, sir," Curtis said.

"What about here?" John pointed to a small cluster of dots, about ten to fifteen miles apart, in Pennsylvania.

"Looks promising. Our analysts flagged it, but that's an industrial complex, so it'll be tricky to search. Not as easy as pulling some data off a computer." The director brushed a hand over his stubble.

Even though things had slowed down recently, he opted to let his facial hair grow a little thicker in these colder months. He stood in contrast to Lieutenant Clarke's clean-shaven features, and Stone's heavy mustache.

"Put together a team, and a list of equipment you'll need—" Van Pierce said, stopping mid-sentence.

Two Army officers entered, followed by three MPs, and crossed the command room to stand in front of Marvin, Curtis, and John. One of the men was tall and lean, the other much shorter, but carrying a stocky, well-muscled build. The rank on their uniforms designated the two men as Lieutenants.

"Director Van Pierce," Baker, the shorter Lieutenant, said. It was more of a statement than a question, addressing the man at the head of the room.

"The one and only," Van Pierce answered.

A brief pause let him know that the men didn't appreciate his casual nature.

"What can I do for you, Lieutenant Baker?" He asked looking at the name on his uniform.

"Orders, sir. Effective immediately, the United States military will be overseeing all Hostile Response Division operations." Baker handed a piece of paper to Marvin.

"You can't do that," Curtis said.

"Not your call, Lieutenant Clarke," the taller officer, Reed, said. "And frankly, it's well above your pay grade, but your ire is duly noted."

"We're with Homeland Security," John said, "not the military."

"HRD is a hybrid branch, having equal jurisdiction within both DHS and the National Guard," Baker said.

Director Van Pierce scanned the paper. His eyes widened, and he glanced at John.

"Your recent operations have resulted in excessive collateral damage, and the significant loss of innocent civilian lives," The stocky officer continued.

"You're lying," John said through gritted teeth.

"Lieutenant Stone," Reed said, "You are to come with us, immediately." The three MPs moved forward, one holding a set of handcuffs. The other two kept their hands empty but held them close to their weapons.

"What's this about? Why are you taking him?" Curtis asked, his anger barely contained.

"By order of the United States Government, we are to remand Lieutenant Stone into custody, under the suspicion of domestic terrorism."

"This is outrageous!" Van Pierce moved in front of John.

The MPs approached the director, who looked the young men up and down, standing his ground. Lieutenant Reed spoke quietly into a radio handset, and two more Military Police entered the room.

John placed a hand on Marvin's shoulder. "It's ok. I'll go with them and find out what's going on."

"Are the cuffs necessary?" Curtis asked.

"I'm sorry, I have no choice," the MP said.

"The hell you don't," Clarke said, stepping around John.

"Don't make us bring you in too, Lieutenant Clarke," Baker said.

"Curtis, stand down. We'll get to the bottom of this," John said.

The cuffs ratcheted onto John's thick wrists, barely securing his arms behind his back. The imposing Ranger was compliant, not wanting to hurt the young MPs, but the three men remained on edge as they escorted him from the room.

Reed addressed the two remaining MPs in the room.

"Escort the Director to his quarters."

Marvin took a step forward. "Escort me to my quarters?"

"You're officially being relieved of command, *Mr.* Van Pierce."

CHAPTER
7

The HRD complex was small, compared to most bases of operation. But significant steps were taken to ensure the facility was secure. The holding cell housing John for the better part of the day had been built to make sure nothing short of a sophisticated explosive device would grant an unauthorized exit.

Now, he sat in an interrogation room, at a steel table bolted to the floor. A thick steel ring was welded onto the top, near John's side, his reinforced steel shackles looped through the ring to make sure he wasn't going to get up without proper permission.

Lieutenant Baker sat in front of John and flipped through the pages of a thick file with narrowed eyes. John noted that it was the stocky man's third pass through the information. He kept his back straight, and his hands on the table, knowing Baker's silence was a tactic to try and gain a psychological advantage over a weak-minded suspect, staying silent so John would have no choice but to break and fill the void.

Several more minutes of silence passed, and Lieutenant Baker inadvertently cleared his throat. He caught himself immediately and glared up at John, who gave a barely perceptible smile. The taller man, Lieutenant Reed, finally entered. He eased the door shut and glanced through the mirror, an amateur move.

"Sorry to keep you waiting, Mr. Stone," Reed said, taking the empty seat next to Lieutenant Baker.

John shifted his gaze to the second man. "I understand. You just needed a little more time to get your lies straight."

Reed smiled, but the uneasiness and tension never left his eyes. "We're just here to get your side of the story."

"And what story is that?"

"Early November, you reported that a team of Russian mercenaries staged an ambush during one of your operations, detonating a series of explosives that killed several HRD operatives."

John narrowed his eyes. "That is correct." He didn't offer any further details, knowing everything would have already been in the report.

"Only days later, and you were in the vicinity of another building, inside which these, *mercenaries*, also detonated explosives, leveling the building in a similar manner." Reed flipped the top sheet of Baker's report to one side, reading the second page.

John locked his eyes on the tall man, dipped his chin in a small nod, then looked at him from under his brows.

Reed turned the second page over, setting it face down on the first while scanning the final page. He took in a breath through his nostrils, and let out a low whistle.

"The same explosives were used for both buildings," Lieutenant Reed said.

"If you say so," John said, keeping his words clipped.

Reed raised an eyebrow, and Baker's mouth pulled into a half sneer.

"Did you think we wouldn't find the rest?" Reed asked.

John sat back slightly, confused by the question. "The rest of what?"

Baker pulled another file from his briefcase and slapped it on the table, whipping the cover open. John looked down at the pictures inside. The top one was a photo taken inside his Montana home. He reached for the file, but just as his fingertips reached the edge, the chains on his shackles pulled taut. John pulled the folder closer with his fingers and picked up the photo.

It showed his kitchen table covered in wires, tools, batteries, digital timers, and pre-paid cell phones. He set the photo aside and looked down at the rest of the stack, spreading them out on the table.

"I'm not sure what kind of terrorist attacks you were planning, Stone, but you're going down for this." Reed poked a finger at one of the pictures.

John stared down, leaning back to take in the photos showing the explosives and equipment scattered around his home. He was being set up to take the fall for something, or someone.

"Who are you really working for?" John asked.

Lieutenant Baker smiled, showing a mouth full of too-small teeth. "We work for the citizens of the United States, John. We're saving American lives, by bringing down a potential terrorist. They're gonna string you up for this."

"You'll be moved immediately to a detention center, where no one will be able to help you, much less find you," Reed said, his voice strangely calm.

John pulled the chains of his shackles tight, and he balled his hands into fists, the knuckles turning red, then ghost white.

CHAPTER 8

"You're restricted to your quarters until further notice, Mr. Van Pierce," the MP said. "A guard will be posted nearby in case you need anything."

"To make sure I don't leave, you mean," Marvin said. "This is absurd. None of this makes sense, does it? Why would they arrest Stone?"

"I'm just following orders, sir."

He shook his head and gave the young soldier a solemn look before stepping into his room and closing the door behind him. John had been taken into custody, and he needed to find out the reason. Van Pierce sat at his desk and opened the laptop, typing a message to Dr. Spencer. He hit send, then sat on his bed, and thumped the back of his head lightly against the wall.

A discussion started just outside his door. The young MP spoke with someone else, and Marvin recognized the other voice. He got up and opened the door.

"Lieutenant Clarke, come in."

"I'm sorry, sir, he—"

"You said I was confined to my quarters, son. You didn't receive any orders to keep anyone else out."

The guard closed his eyes, too afraid of making the wrong call. "Five minutes. Then you've got to go, Lieutenant."

"Thanks, kid," Curtis said, stepping past him into the room.

"How's it going out there?" Marvin asked.

"I was walking with Miranda when got your message. She said you didn't want her to call you, just in case."

"Is she doing what I asked?"

"Yes, sir. She's on her way to give Parker the news. Are we going to find out where John is?"

"I'm not sure if you should," Van Pierce said. "If you start raising suspicion, they'll probably round us all up."

He pressed a knuckle to his lips, thinking about their options. "You need to keep up the perception that you're still following orders. That means you should probably get back to your team soon."

Curtis looked at Marvin, clenching and unclenching his jaw.

"What is it? Why did you come here to talk to me?"

"Do you think John did what they're saying?" Curtis asked.

"I don't believe it for a second," Marvin said. "John was instrumental in taking Warren Ratcliffe down."

"Why would the Army arrest him?" Curtis asked. "Why would they charge him with domestic terrorism?"

Van Pierce pressed his lips together. "I don't know. I just don't know."

✻ ✻ ✻

Dr. Miranda Spencer moved down the hall as fast as she dared without arousing suspicion. She turned the corner and walked into the small room set up as a secondary computer lab.

"Parker."

The programmer raised his eyebrows. "Oh hey, Miranda. What's up?"

"They took John," She said, her voice just above a whisper. She crossed the room and sat next to him.

"Who took him? Where?"

"The Army sent some officers to take over. The men in charge had John arrested."

"Arrested? For what?" Parker turned in his chair to face Miranda.

"They said he was a terrorist." She looked down at her hands resting in her lap. "Director Van Pierce wanted me to try and find out what evidence they have on him. He wanted your help."

Parker's mouth hung open, as he sat speechless for a moment. "Of course. Anything," he said, snapping back to his senses.

His fingers flew over the keyboard, pulling up all the records he could find. Text scrolled across his monitor before a window popped up, putting a stop to his progress.

"Huh?"

"What is that?" Miranda asked, pointing to the warning message.

"I can't get into the files I need."

"What do we do now?"

Parker flexed his neck and wrists, cracking the knuckles on one hand. "Well, playing by the rules isn't going to work, so now I'm changing the game."

***

Parker lost himself in the chase. He spent the last hour breaking through firewalls, organizing files, and following any lead he could find. His wrists ached, and tension pulled at all the muscles from his neck to his lower back. He sat back in his chair, wiping a hand over his face and rubbing an eye with his sleeve.

Miranda leaned in, putting a hand on the armrest of his chair. "What did you find?"

Parker didn't respond. He squinted at the screen, scanning through the document quickly to pick out all the relevant information.

"Parker?" Dr. Spencer tapped him on the shoulder.

He turned to look at her, the blood draining from his face. "John is scheduled to be transported from here tomorrow. They're going to fly him out of the country. To a black site detention center."

"Guantanamo Bay?" Miranda asked, also shaken by the news.

"No. Another one." Parker turned back and started another search. "I didn't even know they had more than one."

Miranda stepped away, arms crossed over her stomach. "We need to tell Director Van Pierce. How can they do this?"

"There's only one reason for the government to send you to an off-the-books facility," Parker said. "They're gonna make John disappear."

"How can they—" Miranda's eyebrows furrowed.

"Miranda, I need your help," Parker said, gently grabbing her by the arms. "We need to help him. Stop the transport before he disappears for good."

"Parker, I...I can't. We don't have the proof to stop this from happening." She stepped back as he released his grip on her arms.

"I just need you to buy me some time until we can free him from the holding cells."

"You're talking about breaking him out? If he's being charged with terrorism or treason, do you know what they'll do to us?" Miranda shook her head frantically. "I'm sorry, Parker, but I can't."

"Alright. I shouldn't have asked, I'm sorry." Parker sat back in his chair, grabbing two handfuls of his hair and bringing his elbows together with a frustrated groan. "This is a setup. I can't let them get away with this."

"They'll lock you up with John. Or they'll kill you, Parker."

He swiped his tongue across his bottom lip and spun his chair back to the computer. "You should go, Miranda. You can't risk being here if I get caught."

Miranda started to respond but stopped herself. She closed her eyes and wiped away the start of a tear with her finger. She adjusted her glasses and rested a hand on Parker's shoulder for a second before leaving.

CHAPTER
9

A burly guard jammed his nightstick into John's ribs, shoving him into the back of an armored van, his hands cuffed behind his back. He still wore the same black t-shirt and dark gray BDU pants from the night before, in the interrogation room.

The muscular guard stepped in with him, holding the nightstick he used to prod John tightly in his fist. They sat across from each other on the steel benches bolted inside the truck. The man wasn't dressed like Military Police. John figured him for homeland security, who generally got their hands on all the domestic terror suspects.

He had no idea where they were about to transport him, but the terrorism charges meant at some point they would be locking him up in a supermax prison, or an undisclosed detention facility, like GitMo.

The vehicle rocked, as the driver and passenger doors slammed shut. The sounds echoed through the mostly concrete motor pool of the Hostile Response Division base of operations.

A deep scowl twisted the guard's features. John didn't know if this was how the man treated all the people he transported, but it was clear the guard didn't think too highly of him.

The big van rumbled to life, and lurched forward, taking John to an uncertain fate.

***

Parker guzzled the last of the energy drink from the can, crushing the tall aluminum cylinder before flinging it into the corner with the other two. His eyes stung, and muscles ached. The hunger and fatigue made it difficult to concentrate, and his hands shook from a combination of too much adrenaline and too much caffeine.

He spent most of the night gathering everything he needed to accomplish his plan and still didn't know how to help John. The most he could do was delay the transport until inspiration struck him. The armored van left the HRD facility ten minutes ago, and Parker needed to get eyes on it. He monitored the progress of the multiple programs he was running, as feeds from a network of various cameras started streaming in.

Tied into the processing cores of the entire HRD computer lab, Parker's computer had almost everything it needed at a moment's notice. It didn't take long to pick up the van transporting John. His programs not only found the vehicle but overlayed likely travel routes, in real-time, based on the driver's patterns.

Parker had another program running to take control of the traffic lights and did his best to stall the progress. *Think, Parker. You can't just sit them at a red light until they pass out from exhaustion.*

His mind raced, and his fingers flew across the keys. He thought about getting the local police to intervene, but making the van run a red light was hardly a cause to call in the SWAT team. Especially not for a DHS transport vehicle.

Maybe an accident severe enough to bring fire and rescue. They wouldn't just leave John in the back if he was in any real danger. Parker pinched the bridge of his nose. An accident that bad would put lives at risk, though. Maybe if one vehicle massive enough hit them, like a big rig. *Or an armored car,* Parker thought, as his eye caught the heavy truck with a bank logo on the side on one of the camera feeds.

The programmer plotted several possible intercept courses, forcing the lights to cooperate, trying to make the two meet. Every attempt resulted in failure. At one point the two vehicles were traveling in the same direction on parallel roads.

Parker turned his chair away from the keyboard and pulled several deep breaths in through his nose, letting the air out through his mouth. "You can do this, Parker."

He opened his eyes again and spun back to the laptop.

CHAPTER
10

John rotated his hands, working the circulation through his wrists again. He leaned back and looked at the guard with him. "This is a setup, you know." Why not open up with the truth.

"Shut up, Stone."

"I didn't detonate those bombs. All of the civilians trapped inside made it into the lab below—"

"I said be quiet," the man said, standing up. He placed his hand on the ceiling to steady himself as the van came to a stop.

"You crossed the wrong people, Stone." The DHS agent's mouth twisted into a sadistic smile. This man was part of the plan. He pointed his nightstick at John.

"They tell me to bring in some piece of garbage that attacked my fellow Americans, and that's what I do." His mock patriotic tone irked the Army Ranger.

John knew once they got him to the detention facility, there would be no chance of proving his innocence. A place like that didn't cater to the fantasy of a trial by jury. He was already guilty in their minds.

The van started to move again, then jerked to a stop. The driver slammed on the brakes and leaned into the horn. Simultaneously, a second horn blared outside, growing louder. John and the guard were launched to one side, as a massive force struck the armored van from the right.

John's body struck the steel side wall, and a jolt of pain tore across his shoulder blades, down his arms, all the way through his fingers. The DHS agent rag dolled against the hard wall, next to him. The van rocked sideways onto two of its wheels, and balanced precariously at the tipping point, before finally landing back on all four wheels. They were tossed by the impact again, this one lessened by the heavy shocks of the van.

They were stopped in the middle of the intersection, and John could hear people outside yelling. The guard finally stood with a sneer, shaking his head to regain his senses.

John bolted into action. He turned his body and dug a boot into the diamond tread floor. With a hard thrust, he dropped low and drove a massive shoulder into the man's body, flattening him up against the opposite wall. The audible crack of ribs giving out sounded, as the DHS agent let out a low huff.

The guard shouted in fury and pain, swinging his nightstick in a wide arc. John, hands still cuffed behind him, leaned his body away and turned his head just enough for the weapon whip by and miss by centimeters. The momentum carried him back against the wall, and the big guard prepared to deliver a backhanded follow-up swing. John launched off the steel surface, dipped his chin and drove his head into the guard's face.

Taking a step back, John watched a line of saliva drip from the man's lips. The guard fell to one knee, and he let the nightstick clatter to the steel floorplate. His hand reached for the pistol on his hip, and he looked up at Stone with pure fire and hatred.

John brought his knee up and thrust a heavy boot forward, ringing the man's head off of the steel door before he dropped unconscious.

***

Parker heard heavy boot steps rushing down the hall. He turned to face the door just as it came crashing in. A pair of men stepped in, pistols drawn.

"Away from the computer!" A young soldier advanced, keeping his weapon pointed at Parker.

He raised his hands. "I'm unarmed. I won't resist." His heart hammered in his chest

"Hands on your head," the lead man said, now only ten feet away.

Parker complied, lacing his fingers together. The soldier kept the gun drawn and used his off hand to force Parker to turn. He pushed the programmer face first against a wall and kicked his feet out past shoulder width.

"Room secure," the other soldier said into his radio.

"I just wanted to help John," Parker said.

"That was stupid," the first soldier said, checking him for weapons. "That's the court's job, not ours."

"John's being framed. Someone at the top is setting him up to take the fall."

Parker's chest hit the wall as the younger soldier pushed a hand on his back, forcing one arm behind him. "And now you're going to end up in the cell right next to Stone, once they find him."

The cuffs clacked into place locking Parker's wrists. *Once they find him?* Another wave of relief washed over him. *He got away.*

***

Shoulders aching, John searched the guard's belt with his hands still cuffed behind his back. He found the keys and freed himself, just as someone slapped the rear door and unlatched it.

"You okay in there, Corey?" the man asked, pulling the door open.

John's snatched the Beretta M9 from the guard's holster. Sunlight spilled into the van, and he brought the pistol up, holding the front sight on the second guard's chest. The man held one hand up but gripped his slung rifle a little tighter.

"Easy, Stone. No one needs to get hurt."

"Let go of the weapon," John said, dropping to the asphalt. He locked eyes with the older guard. "I'm innocent."

"Not if you continue this. Let the courts decide, John."

"The people setting me up don't plan on letting it get that far," John said, circling around the man. "Let's go. Keep looking forward."

The scene was all confusion and chaos. An armored car had struck the van transporting John in the middle of the intersection. He saw several other vehicles also were also involved in collisions, and all four directions still showed green lights.

"Move." John prodded the guard ahead.

"Please, John. There's nowhere to run."

The driver of the armored van spotted the pair moving away. Still dizzy from the accident, he drew his pistol and everyone around him scattered. John turned at the sounds of people screaming and saw the staggering driver pointing a gun at him.

The pistol bucked twice before the guard steadied himself, grabbing the gun with both hands. John tackled the old guard, to keep him from getting shot by the wild firing, then bolted away from the crowd. Three more cracks rang out, kicking up bits of asphalt. John tore ahead, and hopped a low fence, leading to an alley.

He emerged from the alley, running into the street in a full run, too late to see an oncoming car. Tires screeched as the driver slammed the brakes. John tucked his body just before the impact. His back hit the windshield hard enough to force the air from his lungs and spiderweb the glass. The pistol flew from his grasp, and John tumbled down the hood onto the street, dazed.

The driver jumped out of his car, showing a hint of concern, but anger took over as the man started shouting obscenities when he saw John get back on his feet.

"Are you nuts, man? You're paying for this!" the driver yelled, jabbing a finger into John's chest.

"Yeah, I'm really sorry about all of this."

"You're gonna be, you—"

John's fist connected with a slapping thud and the fat man crumpled to the ground. He rushed to the car and slid into the driver's seat. John shifted to reverse and peeled away, executing a sloppy bootleg turn.

Getting rusty, he thought.

He pressed the accelerator down, and the car protested, but somehow managed to get past the speed limit. John would be able to put some distance between himself and his captors, but this car would stand out, even if the driver didn't report it stolen. He had to secure transportation and make it into hiding before whoever was calling the shots put him on the most wanted list.

CHAPTER
11

Miranda stepped into Van Pierce's quarters. "They've arrested Parker."

Marvin looked past her to make sure the guard wasn't too close before he closed the door. He shushed Dr. Spencer and walked her over to a chair to sit down.

"They're going to lock him up in Guantanamo," she said.

"Doctor Spencer, slow down. I don't know what's happening right now."

Miranda set a bag on the desk, tucking the stethoscope inside. Saying she needed to monitor Van Pierce's vitals was the easiest way to convince the guard in the hall to let her see him. She took a long deep breath and continued.

"Parker tried to help free John while they were transporting him, but someone noticed the suspicious computer network activity, so the security forces started searching the building."

Marvin closed his eyes and sighed. "That kid is too reckless with his methods. Is John still on his way to the supermax facility?"

Miranda shook her head putting her glasses back on. "I don't know. No one is telling me anything."

He sighed pressing his hands together. "Yeah, I'm in the same boat."

"We need to get you out of here, sir."

"No. Not yet." Marvin walked to the door and leaned close, listening for any activity outside. "I don't want to arouse any suspicion that could get you in trouble too."

"We can't just let whoever is doing this get away with it," Miranda said. "I can call someone. Maybe there's a chance that—"

"Just stay close to Curtis," Van Pierce said. "I trust his judgment. If there's anything that can be done, he'll be able to do it, and you'll be in the best position to help out."

Dr. Spencer folded her arms across her stomach, leaning forward in the seat. "I guess you're right. I know Lieutenant Clarke is already asking about John, so hopefully, he has some more information already."

"Thank you, Doctor." Marvin opened his door to let Miranda out into the hall just as the young MP walked by.

"All finished, Doctor?" the man asked.

"Yes. Mr. Van Pierce is fine." Miranda tucked the small bag full of medical equipment under her arm and gave him a nod, walking out.

***

The last of the sun's warm glow faded. John ditched the stolen car an hour earlier, heading deep into the city on foot. This late in the year the cold air bit deep into his flesh, seeping into his muscles and bones. He rubbed his arms with cold hands, blowing into them to warm them as best he could. John needed to find shelter, and escape the freezing weather. It wouldn't be long before the city would start seeing snowfall.

To keep his mind off of the chill, John took stock of his equipment and intel. All he had on him was a pair of boots, BDU pants, and a black t-shirt. John always kept some cash stuffed into one of his socks, just above the ankle, for emergencies. He was grateful for that bit of preparation.

The only information he had available was the false trail Baker and Reed used to set him up. They tried to pin three separate explosions on him, and brand him as a terrorist.

This had to go higher than Ratcliffe. Everything John and Curtis had obtained about the man had already been turned over to the HRD analysts. Except for the quick searches that Parker ran. He recalled a name the programmer found, something that stood out in his mind. Kevin Dalling.

John didn't know how he was connected to all of this, but it was the only thread within reach. And he intended to tug at the loose end, seeing what else would spill out as it all unraveled.

Fighting the numbness in his arms, John pushed forward, staggering out into the night. If he was going to find out how Dalling fit into all of this, he needed internet access.

The nearest library would be his best bet. It would be closed this time of night so he would have to wait until the morning. Until then, the idea of tucking himself into the back corner of a diner, with a hot coffee between his hands was appealing enough to outweigh the risk of someone spotting him.

CHAPTER
12

Pryce Windham pressed his thumb and middle finger into his temples, listening to the man on the other end of the call.

"He escaped, sir. Uh, Stone escaped."

"Yes, I got that part," Pryce said, fighting to keep his voice steady and calm. "Can you please go over the rest of the details again, Senator Wales?"

"Yeah. Yeah, so, the van was on its way to bring John Stone to the maximum security facility when an armored car ran a red light."

Pryce waited for several seconds for the caller to continue. "And that's it? The armored car hit the van so hard Stone disappeared?"

"No, sir. I was just looking at the reports, and something didn't make sense," Byron Wales said. *"After the accident, John was able to subdue the guard inside, taking his weapon. From there he held a second man at gunpoint until he had the*

opportunity to flee. The driver fired his weapon, trying to stop Stone, but he was able to get away."

"Maybe I'm missing something, but that all seems to make some semblance of sense," Pryce said. "I see a clear case of incompetence."

"Uh, what I mean, sir, is that the armored car didn't run a red light. The accident reports state that every vehicle involved in the accident claimed that their respective lights were green. Someone tampered with the traffic lights."

"I'm aware of that, Senator. My people have already handled the situation."

"Of course, Mr. Windham. What is it you would like me to do, then?" the senator asked.

"What I need from you, Byron, is to tap into your state's resources and initiate a manhunt." Pryce leaned into the senator's first name, the lack of any title meant to communicate a clear hierarchy in their relationship.

"John Stone is a federal fugitive. I can't just pull men and women off of their assigned duties without a clear order from a higher agency, to look for someone that doesn't appear in any criminal database."

"If Stone shows up on a most wanted list, and the FBI get him before I do, that would complicate our arrangement, Byron. Is that what you really want?"

Senator Wales sighed on the other end, pausing for a moment. *"It's getting too heavy, Windham. I need to take a step back. I need some breathing room."*

"What was that, Senator?" Pryce sat back in his chair, struggling to keep the frustration out of his words.

"I need to distance myself from you, Mr. Windham. For a little while at least, until this all blows over."

"As long as John Stone is free, there is no *blowing over*," Pryce said. "He can bring the whole thing down on our heads."

"It's your operation he's threatening, Pryce," the senator said.

Pryce was taken aback. He spent a few seconds to collect himself, before continuing. "If you think for one moment that none of this will blow back on you, my friend, you are sorely mistaken."

"I've taken steps to protect myself," the senator said, his bravado growing. *"I've got a file stashed away that can help clear my name, and my conscience."*

"You think that file will keep you safe?" Pryce's words dripped with anger.

There was a long pause on the other end. *"If something were to happen to me,"* Wales said, *"copies of the file will start turning up at every major news outlet in the country. In the world."*

"Very well, Senator. We can play this your way," Pryce said, smoothing his hair back and straightening his tie. "You can have your space, but remember when this is all over, I will not forget your veiled threat against me. There will be a reckoning."

"Mr. Windham, I—"

Pryce killed the call and closed his eyes, rubbing his temple as he took several deep breaths. He stood up and buttoned his jacket, walking around his desk where Mr. Gordon stood, listening to the call. He put a hand on the enforcer's shoulder.

"I need you to clean this up."

"Yes, sir. I'll start the search for Stone right away."

"No," Pryce said. "I'm talking about Senator Wales. This file he's talking about is a liability. One that I'm not comfortable with leaving unaddressed. You must find out what he's got, and where he is keeping it. No loose ends."

Mr. Gordon nodded, a slow, deliberate movement, and turned to leave. "Understood. Consider it done."

CHAPTER
13

Curtis kept his eyes forward as he walked down the hall toward Director Van Pierce's quarters. The man he was looking for spotted him and approached.

"Can I help you, Lieutenant?" the MP asked.

The young man had been posted in this section of the HRD base when the takeover occurred. Curtis didn't trust him yet, but his intuition about the man told him to take a chance.

"I need to get this to the director," Curtis said.

He held out the envelope, hoping his gut hadn't steered him wrong. He could see in the man's eyes he was torn. The MP knew something was off, by the way everyone in the base had been acting. Many of the HRD staff went along with the government officials coming in, but some felt it was an unnecessary action or even a blatant overreach that hurt their effectiveness. The morale in the base had waned, and if Curtis didn't read this kid right, he was about to make things worse.

"I'll see that he gets it, Lieutenant Clarke." He took the envelope reluctantly, averting eye contact.

"Thank you, Private," Curtis said. "This is urgent. It's about John Stone."

His eyes went to Curtis at the mention of John's name. He hesitated, almost handing the package back. "I shouldn't be doing this. Delivering this to Mr. Van Pierce, I mean."

"You know as well as I do, something strange is happening," Curtis said, softening his expression. "I'm just trying to find out what the hell is going on, and how I can help." He pointed at the paper in the man's hand. "Can I count on you?"

The man stared down at the envelope, biting his lower lip in thought. "Yes. I'll make sure Mr. Van Pierce gets it."

"Thank you," Curtis said with a nod.

* * *

"When did Lieutenant Clarke give this to you?" Marvin asked, taking the envelope.

"He just left, sir. Maybe two minutes ago."

"Thanks, son. No one else knows about this?"

The MP shook his head. "No, sir. I brought it to you as soon as I finished my last round."

Marvin nodded and closed the door. He walked to his desk and tore the flap of the envelope open, pulling out a single folded sheet of paper. Curtis' handwriting filled half of the page, scrawled in a hurry.

He spent several minutes reading and rereading the report, eyes narrowed. Curtis included as much information he could about John escaping during transit. It wasn't known how it happened, but Parker's arrest was also covered, mentioning that he had been arrested for aiding a fugitive.

After that, Curtis wrote that he would be part of the team tasked with bringing John back. It was the best way to make sure John returned alive so they could find out the truth. Curtis didn't know or trust John as well as Marvin did, but he still had a great deal of respect for the man.

Someone was setting John up to take the fall. Marvin didn't have a suspect in mind, and the uncertainty of it all put him on edge.

* * *

Miranda Spencer left the briefing room after talking to Curtis about everything they currently knew. A voice addressed her from behind, and she turned to see Lieutenant Reed walking toward her.

"Can I have a word, Doctor?"

"Of course, Lieutenant," she said, keeping her composure. "I was headed to the lab. Just wanted to talk to the analysts about the data crunching."

Reed's eyebrows raised almost imperceptibly. "Oh, did no one tell you? That has been put on hold after Mr. Lewis commandeered the network for his private use."

Miranda had already known the analysts were told to stand down, but she played coy, not wanting to tip her hand. Reed asking to talk was a sign that they did have their suspicions, however.

"This way," the lieutenant gestured for Dr. Spencer to follow him to a different room.

She followed, her footsteps creating a mismatched rhythm that almost harmonized, three steps for every two Reed took. Neither spoke, as they rounded a corner and reached an already opened door. Reed motioned for her to enter. Miranda saw Lieutenant Baker already seated, a laptop in front of him and a small stack of papers shuffled about on the table.

She smoothed her lab coat and skirt along the back of her thighs, taking a seat on the opposite side. Reed closed the door and joined Baker, sitting further back from the long table.

Miranda broke the silence. "What can I do for you two?"

Baker looked up from his display as a smile spread across his round face. What would typically be a comforting expression now had a hint of smugness. Like he was winning. Miranda took a deep breath through her nose, pursing her lips and fidgeting in her chair.

"Doctor Spencer, we just want to ask you a few questions about your time with John Stone over the past couple of months," Baker said, letting the smile fade as he got back to business.

"Yes, of course. What about it?" Miranda placed her hands in her lap. She sat up straight and looked the man in the eye.

Baker let the moment stretch as he casually scratched at a nonexistent itch on his cheek. "How long have you worked with Mr. Stone?"

"Uh, like you mentioned, a couple of months."

"Can you give us an exact date, please, Doctor."

"Not off the top of my head, no," Miranda said. "I only just met him, like seven or eight weeks ago. That's when Director Van Pierce—"

"Mr. Van Pierce has been relieved of duty," Reed said, interrupting. "He is no longer the acting director of this facility."

"Sorry. That's when Mr. Van Pierce introduced me to John." Miranda's voice started to waver.

"Were you aware of John Stone's plans to execute a number of terrorist attacks across the United States?" Baker read the question with no emotion, like someone reading the ingredients on a box of cereal.

"What?"

Baker's eyes moved up, peering at Miranda over the paper. "Were you aware that John Stone planted explosives in two separate buildings, killing US citizens. Or that he had plans to execute more?"

"He didn't plant any explosives." Miranda had her hands on the table, leaning forward.

"Six weeks ago, John Stone detonated a series of explosives, killing half a dozen Hostile Response Division agents. Your own team, Doctor Spencer." A hint of Baker's smile returned.

"That wasn't John," Miranda said.

"Days later, he detonated another explosive device that brought an entire building down. Casualty reports say three civilians died and almost three dozen injured as a result," Reed said, stepping forward.

"That's not true! He saved those people. All of them. John is the reason they made it to that reinforced lab in the basement." Miranda folded her arms across her stomach and straightened her posture.

"Witness accounts say that he entered the building, fully armed and holding a detonator," Baker said. "When the device failed to explode, the people fled downstairs to avoid him."

"That's not what happened!" Miranda was shouting now, ready to leap up from her chair.

The blatant lying set her off. Only when it was too late did she realize that was the reaction Baker was looking for. His crooked grin waxed and waned as the man fought to maintain his composure.

"What about Parker? He was there. So was Ty," She said.

"Parker Lewis? You mean the man we just arrested for aiding in Stone's escape?" Reed asked, standing at one end of the table now.

"Tae Seung Min, known by his alias, Ty Octane." Baker read the name off of a separate sheet. "This man has a criminal record and is known to participate in illicit and illegal activities. We're supposed to take the accounts of these two seriously?"

Reed came back with his *good cop* demeanor. "Please, Doctor. We are only asking for your help to bring John in before anyone else gets hurt."

"I don't know where he is." Miranda's voice was barely above a whisper. She spoke the truth, and it almost relaxed her to say it.

"But you know how Parker works. His methods may prove useful to track down Stone," Baker said.

"Can I talk to Parker? I'll convince him to help."

"I'm sorry, that's not possible," Reed said. "Perhaps you can just explain to us how Mr. Lewis used his software to find the targets the HRD was hunting."

"Don't you have his computer? Can't you just use the programs he wrote?"

Baker's face betrayed him, as a flash of frustration washed over his features. "Mr. Lewis is an, unconventional software engineer. Our team can't make sense of what's on there."

Miranda felt the situation shift back in her favor. Parker's quirky programming style frequently frustrated her, but now it was helping. Lieutenant Reed also noticed the shift and poured on the pressure.

"Doctor, if you refuse to help, I'm afraid you will be detained and possibly charged with aiding and abetting a known fugitive," he said. "Helping terrorists looks very bad in the court's eyes."

"I don't know how it works, though," she said, shrinking down.

"Maybe if you can just tell us *what* it does, we can figure out the rest," Reed said, slipping back into a friendly tone again. "Why does he tap into the camera recordings?"

"None of them are real-time, and the footage isn't usable for any facial recognition software," Baker added.

Miranda flitted her gaze back and forth between the two. "It's for tracking movement," she said. "And predicting where a target will go."

"How does he accomplish that?" Baker asked, writing down notes.

Miranda stared down at her hands, having felt like she just betrayed her entire team.

"Doctor," Reed said. "Please. Maybe you can help us find John."

She shook her head as a tear streamed down her cheek. "I can't. I don't know how the mob recognition program works."

"Mob recognition?" Baker wrote something down and leaned in closer. "What does that do?"

"I—I can't."

Reed's hand rested on her shoulder now. "Doctor Spencer, what does Parker's mob recognition software do? If you can help us, we will take all of that into account and show leniency on your team.

Van Pierce, Parker, even John. Please, doctor, will you help us?"

Miranda pressed a hand to her mouth, eyes red and shoulders shaking. She looked up and nodded to Lieutenant Reed.

CHAPTER
14

John sat at one of the library computers, rubbing warmth into his fingers. Early morning sunlight streamed through the windows, but his mind was clouded from fatigue. He stayed awake through the night, gathering his thoughts and keeping an eye out for anyone tracking him down.

One name, Kevin Dalling, was all John had to work with. He didn't know who the man was, or even if he had a significant connection to the person setting him up. Parker found the name while sifting through the data they found, in the hands of the mercenaries Curtis Clarke's team had taken down.

John would have to pinpoint a location for Dalling, to start his hunt for the man trying to frame him. His first priority, however, was to look through all the major and local news sites, trying to find out if word of his escape had spread to law enforcement.

It took him the better part of an hour, looking at all the major sites, and then doubling back in case any of them had been updated with new information while he was busy on another site. Though John was branded a terrorist by the men that had him arrested, nothing about him, the car accident, or even his escape had been reported anywhere.

They're hiding it, John thought. The people orchestrating this whole thing don't want anyone to know. That meant it had to be a small group within the government or someone with strong ties to that group. The situation was both a blessing and a curse. If Homeland Security were actually involved, his name would have appeared everywhere, with warnings being broadcast nationwide. Now he could operate a little more freely, knowing not everyone was on the lookout for him. On the other hand, someone powerful enough to suppress any news about John would have plenty of resources at his disposal.

John smiled. He rocked the boat, and someone needed him, and the HRD, out of the picture, before they could discover who that was. He needed to seize the initiative and press the attack now. Good men and women died as a result of this shadow group's actions, and John was about to bring the entire organization down.

"Let's see what you can do for me, Kevin," John said, scrolling through the search results.

Parker's mystery man was connected to several high-profile clients. Many of them were in government roles, although the majority seemed to be entrepreneurial types. John had two options to pursue, the government or the business connections. Focusing on the Senators, Governors, and other influential people could bring too much heat down on him.

It would be harder to put pieces together chasing the business leads, but targeting mostly fraudulent companies would garner less notice by the public. John sketched out the suspected names and locations on small scraps of paper, using the stubby pencil the library provided. Now he had a list of probable target locations to search, but given his limited resources, their proximity also had to factor into his decision. That singled out one particular building to start his search. The *Essential Eye*, a small design firm only a couple hundred miles from him, was his next destination.

"Next stop, Colorado."

CHAPTER
15

Morgan Dowd closed the door behind him, kicking his shoes off as he entered his apartment. He hung his bag up on a hook and shrugged his coat off, unwrapping the light scarf from around his neck. He twisted his head to one side, letting the stretch run down one side of his neck.

"Need a chiropractor?"

"Jesus!" Morgan fell back, knocking his coat rack down, clutching his chest. "Who are you?"

Mr. Gordon sat at the kitchen table, slicing another chunk off of an apple and taking a bite. He flipped the small kitchen knife, blade down in an ice pick grip and slammed it into the wooden surface. The menacing enforcer stood up and tossed the rest of the apple into the sink and wiped his hands with a dishtowel.

"That's not important, Mr. Dowd. You only need to know that I'm here on behalf of Byron Wales. I understand that you are in possession of a certain file."

"The Senator? What does he want with me?" Morgan asked keeping his back pressed against the wall as he stood up.

Mr. Gordon tilted his head and smiled. A crooked smile that leaned to one side. "I think you're not grasping why I'm here. Senator Wales didn't send me. My employer asked that I stop by and straighten some things out. You are a journalist, are you not?"

Morgan picked the coat rack up and fumbled for his messenger bag. "I don't know what you're talking about. I'm going to call the police." He found the phone in the side pouch of the bag and looked up to see the man in his kitchen unbuttoning his overcoat, letting it fall open and revealing a pistol holstered in his waistband.

"We got off on the wrong foot," Gordon said. "Let me start over. I'm here on behalf of Senator Byron Wales, to ask that you do not release a particular file that would," he waved a hand tracing small circles in the air as he searched for the word, "complicate matters for my employer."

"Y-You work for Pryce Windham?" Morgan let his arm drop, still clutching the phone.

"My, you certainly are good at your job," Mr. Gordon said, raising his eyebrows. "That saves me time dancing around hinting at why you need to hand over those files."

Morgan shook his head. "I don't know who told you that I'm somehow involved, but they're wrong. I'm not part of the Senator's plans."

"That's unfortunate. You see, Mr. Dowd, after this discussion here, I'm going to drive across town to visit your mother." The enforcer snapped the blade of his tactical folder open and closed, in a hypnotic tick-tock rhythm.

Morgan's face grew pale. His jaw dropped open, and his heart raced. Fear filled his eyes.

"It won't take long. I may even have time to visit your sister, Casey. She's only about ten minutes from your mother's place, right?"

Morgan covered his mouth with his hand. A tear fell down his face, running over the contours of his fingers.

"Your niece should be in the middle of finishing up her homework or helping set the table for dinner by the time I arrive. Maybe they'll even fix a plate for me."

"P-Please. She's only eight."

Mr. Gordon narrowed his eyes. "Well," he stretched the word out, before continuing. "I suppose if you turn the files over, I would have to bring them back to my employer. It wouldn't leave me enough time to visit your family."

The phone fell from Morgan's hand, clattering on the hardwood floor. "I can't. Those files aren't mine to give."

Crossing the kitchen in three smooth strides, Mr. Gordon hoisted the man by his neck and pressed him against the wall. All pretense of politeness was gone. "If you don't hand over those files, I'll kill everyone you know and love, ensuring the information never sees the light of day."

Morgan clutched Gordon's wrists with his hands, struggling to support his weight.

"I'll leave a trail of death and destruction in my wake. One that you had the power to prevent, Mr. Dowd." He dropped the journalist.

Morgan fell to all fours, coughing and gagging.

"So what shall it be?" Windham's enforcer crouched next to the man. "The easy way, or the fun way?"

* * *

"It's all here, then?" Mr. Gordon asked, clutching the small paper between his index and middle finger. "All of the files are located here?"

"Yes," Morgan said, clutching his throat, voice still raspy.

"Digital and hard copies?"

The journalist nodded.

"And you are certain that no other copies exist? If I even catch a hint of this story in your paper," he let his words hang.

"No other copies," Morgan said. "Wales didn't want to risk it getting out unless something happened to him. He was very explicit in his instructions."

"Excellent. I truly appreciate your help."

Mr. Gordon turned as if he were going to leave.

Morgan took a step forward, wanting to ask, but daring not to speak. *Does this mean you won't kill me, or my fam—*

The enforcer whipped his body around, and his right leg lashed out, executing a crisp spinning heel kick. The foot landed flush against Morgan's temple. His skull cracked, and his head snapped viciously to the side, under the force of Mr. Gordon's augmented speed and strength.

Morgan twisted and slammed against the wall before his body crumpled. He was dead before he hit the floor. Mr. Gordon stood on one foot with his kicking leg still in the air. He brought his knee in an swiped a hand down his shin to straighten his pant leg before setting it back down.

He dialed his phone, holding it to his ear as he memorized the information on the small slip of paper in his hand.

"I've got the location of the files. I'm just finishing up here."

Mr. Gordon ended the call and slipped the phone back into his jacket pocket. He knelt next to a small duffel bag he left in the kitchen earlier and pulled out several small cylindrical devices, setting them in various locations in the kitchen, where Morgan Dowd's body lay.

He left the duffel bag on the floor, tucked a remote detonator into his other pocket, and put his gloves back on. He looked both directions down the hall as he left, making sure no one saw him. On his way out the front of the building, Mr. Gordon plucked the fire alarm handle, setting it off as he thumbed the button on the detonator.

The incendiary devices in Morgan's kitchen devoured everything inside. A plume of thick black smoke belched out of the opened window of his apartment.

It took Gordon five minutes of walking to reach his car. As he drove away, he passed two fire trucks heading to the apartment building to battle the blaze. *Not a bad response time for rush hour,* he thought.

CHAPTER
16

John thanked the man driving the old pickup as he hopped out of the truck's cluttered bed. It took most of the day, hitchhiking to reach his destination. By the time John crossed the city limits, it was well past sundown. The only sleep he had were the few moments stolen in the biting wind, bouncing around in the bed of a pickup truck, or slouched in the back of a utility van.

The Essential Eye office was closer to the center of the small city in northern Colorado, but lucky for John, his last ride was *passing through* and dropped him off close enough to check the place out. He rubbed his hands up and down his arms then took stock of his possessions. He bought a flash drive and prepaid phone before arriving, using up a good chunk of his cash. No tools, no weapons, and no backup. *No problem.*

John reached the building by 2 a.m. It was a small compared to larger, multi-story facilities, but the business didn't need to be large to channel a lot of money through for laundering. It was considered a high-end design boutique, catering to several large clients. Or at least that's what it said on paper. John knew that Dalling used this as one of the hubs for cleaning money from a large part of someone's shady network. He just needed to follow the money. It would, no doubt, lead him to the top of the food chain at some point.

The design firm was among several other buildings within a prominent shopping center. The big box stores ate up much of the real estate, all connected in one long line of logos and a vast parking lot. The rest was filled in with smaller single-establishment buildings and a few longer ones with several businesses next to one another.

A security guard was driving around monitoring the entire shopping complex, but two men were tasked explicitly to patrol the Essential Eye office. One man roamed around inside, walking a set pattern, and a second guard outside watched the entrance. These two were professionals, not the typical rent-a-stars.

John watched from deep shadows across the street, trying to find a way into the building. The outside guard would occasionally poke his head inside to make a comment to the other man. Once, he went in to grab a coffee. John noted that each time the man opened the door, he didn't use a key or card. It was unlocked.

"Finally something's going my way," John muttered, blowing into his hands, to keep them warm.

Using the shadows along the bushes, he crept up to the building. At the rear entrance, he flattened his back against the wall next to the security door, waiting for the outside guard to restart his circuit. John glanced down at the lever of the door. *There's no way this is unlocked.* He tugged lightly and smiled as it refused to budge.

He saw his opening, when the regular security guard turned a corner, and moved around to the front, hugging the building. John reached the front entrance and saw the shopping center guard talking to the man out front. John was in their field of view, but a shadow helped keep him hidden as he moved. His original plan was to take out the front guard quietly, while the other two weren't around. This distraction was another coincidence working in his favor.

Heart racing, his breath came out in short visible puffs. He held his breath and eased the glass door open, slipping inside. The sound of steps muffled on the short-pile industrial carpet snapped his attention to the interior. The other guard was making his way to the entrance.

John hurried to a dark corner next to a large fake plant, crouching just as the man passed by. The guard opened the front door and shouted to the other two.

"Hey Joe, does Nate want some coffee too? I just put another pot on."

John knew as soon as the guard turned to head in, he would be right in the man's line of sight. There was no way this plastic tree would hide his bulk, even in the low light.

Go now, John, he urged.

He straightened up, and turned the corner smoothly, slipping farther into the offices.

***

Dr. Spencer held one arm across her stomach, bracing the elbow of her other arm up. She paced back and forth, absently chewing on her thumbnail. The team that had taken the HRD facility over brought a couple of their own computer techs, and she was in the lab helping them get Parker's computer up and running.

Both techs, a man, and a woman looked a lot like each other. Almost comically so. They had similar clothing, short sleeve button up shirts with dark ties, and they wore their hair at practically the same length, with the woman's just a bit longer, touching her shoulders.

The man, Daniel, turned in his chair pushing his glasses up. "How long does this normally take?"

Miranda blinked and looked down at him "Hours. It's a lot of data to parse, even if you know where to look."

"No, I meant how long to find the connections to the cameras?" He tapped the display where a progress bar sat, frozen at twelve percent.

She shook her head. "I'm not sure, I was never here for that part. Parker always seemed to have it ready to go."

The man grumbled and turned back to his work, pulling up another window and typing up some notes.

"How did Parker narrow the search?" the woman, Renee, asked.

"Uh, we always had a point of origin," Miranda said. "So if you're looking for John, you would just start at the intersection of the accident. The traffic cameras."

The computer tech closed her eyes, almost annoyed at the answer. "Yes, I realize that. I'm talking about once the target is spotted."

Miranda had to press her lips together to keep from firing back a witty retort. "It's not real-time. You don't narrow the search, it just traces the path for you once the subject is located."

She could see the other woman also struggling to maintain her composure. "What I meant was, how do you pick out specific traits to find your suspect."

This was going to be a long night. Neither one had received any kind of briefing on Parker's mob recognition program, and Miranda didn't have the working knowledge to walk them through it.

"I don't know," she said after a long pause. "The computer runs an analysis through the database looking for the target's traits and the traits of any known associates."

"Great, that's what I'm talking about," Renee said. "How do we find that in this mess?" she gestured to Parker's laptop.

"Well, I'm not sure John's traits were logged into the computer. Also, he's not going to be with anyone, so it will have to pick him out without the additional data points."

"Thank you, Doctor," Daniel said, trying to ease the tension. "Let's get started then."

"How do we get the data we need?" Renee asked before Miranda blurted out the same question.

"We've probably got plenty of mission footage of John Stone. That's got to be enough to build an initial profile." The man took his glasses off, rubbing one of the lenses along the outer edge of his sleeve.

***

There were only half a dozen offices in the building. Most of them contained useless files, design work to maintain the front for a company funneling money through it. Still, it took John over an hour, playing hide-and-seek with the guard inside as he made his way to each door.

He reached the main office in the back and peered around the corner, ensuring the guard wasn't able to see inside. He powered up the display, waking it from its sleep.

The computer was still somewhat new, or the user was pretty strict about keeping the files organized. That was a good thing for John, who didn't want to waste time slogging through an endless ocean of scattered icons on a cluttered desktop.

John took another glance into the hall, to make sure the guard wasn't around. He pulled the flash drive from his pocket and inserted it into the USB port on the side of the monitor. Seconds passed excruciatingly slow, waiting for the computer to recognize the new storage device. Once it finally appeared, John dragged as many files onto the drive as he could. The workstation held much more than the cheap flash drive could contain.

John mouthed a silent curse and looked around the office. He pulled the drawers open, looking for a spare drive, or some other storage device, but found nothing that would help. He had to make the call to pick and choose what he wanted to take with him.

It took several more minutes than he would have liked, but John had the files narrowed down, and copying over to the small drive. The progress bar let him know it would take a few minutes to complete, so he turned the display off and moved to the file cabinets. He quietly pulled the first drawer open and thumbed through the folders until he found a few with names that he recognized from his search in the library.

Most of the papers inside were useless to John, but each of the folders had documents detailing transactions. John wanted minimal exposure here, and taking anything with him could be noticed. He spread the sheets of the first file on the floor, and took the burner phone out to snap pictures. He struggled to get the focus to work in the low light.

Once he was happy with what he saw on the screen, John pressed the button to take the picture. The phone's flash pulsed, filling the office and it let out a simulated shutter click. *Stupid, John. Very stupid.*

"Who's in there?" The guard inside said, sounding closer to the office than John expected.

He was on his feet just as the man pushed the door open. A bright white beam flashed into John's eyes, and he heard the metallic *snik* of a snap baton being deployed.

"Who are you?" The man yelled in surprise.

John put his hands up to block the harsh glare, still holding the mobile phone.

"Say cheese," he said.

"Wha—"

The brilliant flash went off, blinding the guard, followed again by the shutter clicking sound. The man squeezed his eyes shut, and swung his baton in a wild backhanded arc. John leaned away, then stepped through when the weapon cleared. A heavy fist thundered across the man's jaw, and he crashed to the floor in a twisted heap.

John pulled a pair of handcuffs from the guard's belt and snapped one end on a wrist before noticing the jacket he wore. It was made of a light, but sturdy, dark fabric. He pulled the man's arms out of the sleeves and put the coat on. It fit, though it was snug around his chest when zipped up.

He saw the flashlight beam from the second guard through one of the windows. If the other man noticed his buddy wasn't at his post, John would probably have to take him out as well. He pulled the flash drive from the monitor, unsure if all the files had been copied over. John snatched up an armful of hard copies from the drawer, but he had to leave the ones splayed out on the carpet behind.

He took the cap from the unconscious guard, and pulled it low over his head before slipping out the front door. He circled around the building, heading the opposite direction as the second guard made it to the front. John tucked the file folders into his jacket and snuck to the sidewalk before he made his way into the night.

Reaching the corner, John stuffed his cold hands into the jacket's pockets. He felt a small plastic shape in one side, and pulled out a key fob. It was for the guard's car. He looked at the manufacturer logo on the key and saw a couple of cars parked at the far end of the shopping complex lot. A smile pulled at his face as he jogged toward the vehicles.

CHAPTER
17

John parked the car in a dark alley and kept its heater cranked to full. He watched the snow coming down outside, the wind drawing the flakes down in shifting swirling patterns. It was still just a light dusting, but heading back out into the cold didn't sound appealing at all.

Leaving the key in the ignition, John killed the engine, adjusted his hat, and stuffed the files back into his jacket. He stepped outside, and the cold air already stung his face. John noticed a motel and circled back for a couple of miles to find a good place to leave the car. He had to ditch the vehicle, but hopefully, someone with questionable morals would see it and take it for a joy ride, helping to put some distance between the car and where he was headed.

If he started walking now, he would reach the motel just as the sun came up. The thought of stopping at the diner nearby and grabbing a comforting, hot coffee appealed to him. As his stomach growled, John used the image of bacon, eggs, and toast as motivation to keep his feet moving.

He tugged the collar of his jacket up and walked into the darkness.

***

"You awake, Doctor?" Renee asked, tapping Miranda's chair with a foot.

Miranda bolted upright, nearly falling. "What time is it?" She rubbed her eyes and looked around the room.

"Almost eight," Renee said. "Daniel just got a location to start our search, and we need your help to kickstart the whole thing."

"How?"

"By telling us how Parker uses the point of origin to track a target. We're pulling the recordings from cameras in the area now."

"No, I mean how did Daniel get the location?"

Renee gave her a smile that was equal parts frustration and amusement. "We received a call this morning. It seems John hit some random design firm's office late last night?"

"Where?" Miranda stretched and rubbed her arms to fight off the cold, stale air in the lab.

"Colorado." Renee pulled Miranda's chair next to Daniel and gestured for her to sit. "Doctor."

She sat. "Why would John target an office in Colorado?"

"Our's isn't to ask why, only to answer where," Daniel said as his fingers flew over the keys.

"Now please, Doc, let's not waste any more time," Renee said.

Miranda put her glasses on and did her best to fix her hair. "Can you bring up the closest camera footage?"

A window popped up showing John walking through a hallway, putting a hat on his head, but in the image, the brim was high enough for a sliver of light to hit his face. In the back, Miranda could see another man on the floor, dead or unconscious. She couldn't tell which.

"Where is this?"

"The cameras inside the office," Renee said.

"We kind of lucked out on the quality," Daniel said. "We've got his clothes, face, and his exact location at an exact time. Is that enough to start the search?"

Dr. Spencer's heart sank. "Yes. That should be enough." Her voice was low.

She walked them through the process of using the footage to add to the profile they built using John's

HRD mission footage. From there they started the search.

"This is where the fun begins," Daniel said, cracking his knuckles. "Release the hounds."

The computers around the lab lit up, fans whirring, as the networked processors churned through the data passing around. More cameras were added to the search, as the radius widened. Daniel and Renee spoke to each other in hushed tones, pointing to different monitors, windows, and data points. Soon Miranda felt fatigue pulling her back to sleep.

"Got him!" Renee shouted, snapping Miranda back again.

"Where?" Daniel asked, rolling his chair over to the other tech.

"A twenty-four-hour diner. Looks like he had breakfast there about three hours ago." She pointed to one of the displays and scribbled some notes on a pad, rolling over to input the location into their search.

The mob recognition software shifted its priorities, abandoning various queries and shelving most of the stored footage, narrowing its search to the most relevant position.

"Where is he now, though?" Miranda asked, clutching her hands together.

"We don't know that yet," Daniel said, "but Parker's program should find him soon enough. This is pretty interesting stuff, you know?"

"Yeah," Miranda said.

She always felt Parker's methods pushed the boundaries of legality and knew that Director Van Pierce didn't wholly approve. That these two techs were so eager to use it told Miranda that they had no problem operating outside of the boundaries of the law. And she had no choice but to help them.

* * *

John sat on a worn wooden chair in his motel room. The files he took from the Essential Eye were spread out across the bed. He read all the relevant pages, finding the transactions that stood out the most. John turned the small flash drive between his thumb and forefinger, unable to access any of the data without a computer.

A small place, like this motel, didn't have any kind of business center, which limited his options. John got up and tossed the flash drive onto the table, grabbing the notepad and pen to start scribbling a rough web of likely targets and activity, based on the hard copies.

He wasn't able to grab the most important file, but he did have the photo of one of the pages on his burner smartphone. John tapped the screen, swiped past a blurry image of the surprised guard's face, and pulled up the picture he was looking for.

He zoomed on the photo of the document, skimming it at first. He read through the info in detail, but there wasn't enough to point John to the top of the chain of command, though he found enough to steer him in the right direction. Everything in the files directed him toward a second probable location, but John knew that by the time he reached it, the person he was after would know he was at the Essential Eye.

He spent the next twenty minutes scribbling a loose web of connections, based on the frequency and amount of the transactions passing through the design firm. One point, in particular, stood out, a manufacturer that specialized in furnishings for homes and offices. The perfect front to move money in and out of an interior design firm.

The proximity would make it hard for John to reach it quickly. That gave the people behind the setup plenty of time to beef up their security measures. One of the names also connected to the second target caught John's eye. He was sure it was someone affiliated with Warren Ratcliffe. Autin

Pennell, a small-time money man, frequently working with many of the businesses in John's search, including one of Warren's more lucrative operations.

Pennell was somehow tied up in all of this, washing money, no doubt. If he wanted to get to the man at the top, John needed to take great leaps, targeting the connections like this one. John rubbed the fingers of his right hand, thinking about how he could possibly approach the building without any weapons.

"Not like you have much choice, John," he said, leaning back in his chair.

CHAPTER
18

Curtis stepped out of the SUV, as the driver turned off the engine. He had a three-man HRD team with him, tasked with bringing John Stone in. None were part of his usual crew, each man assigned by the new management for HRD, sent to take over command after Van Pierce was relieved of his position as Director. Curtis knew almost nothing about the three soldiers with him, but their attire, mismatched choice of gear, and facial hair suggested that they were private defense contractors. Mercenaries.

"Fan out," Curtis said. "Watch all the exits."

The men brought their rifles up and moved toward the small motel. Patrons saw the armed soldiers approaching and ran back to their rooms, or scrambled for cover. Curtis wanted to let the men know that they didn't need to treat this as an assault, but the truth was, he had no idea if John was armed, or how he would react.

This motel was John's last known position, passed down to him by the two computer techs with Dr. Spencer. Renee sent the coordinates to his team early that morning, and Curtis got them rounded up and moved out.

With the exits covered, Curtis walked into the main office. It was small, with only enough room for a few people to stand at the chest-high counter. An older woman leaned out of the back room trying to watch the mercenaries encroaching on the property. She used the door frame as partial cover when Curtis entered.

"Don't be alarmed, ma'am," he said. "We're not here to hurt anyone. I'm working with the Department of Homeland Security, and we're looking for a suspect." He kept his rifle hanging from its sling, and his pistol holstered.

"I ain't seen anyone suspicious," she said shrinking back.

Curtis knew the woman was nervous about having four armed men on the premises. "I understand, I'm here to ask if you've seen this man."

He pulled out a sheet of paper with two images of John, one from his most recent photo ID, and the other, a still pulled from security camera footage. The older woman looked at the paper, then came out fully behind the counter and leaned closer to get a better look, adjusting her glasses and tilting her head back.

The facial expressions she made bounced between relief and confusion. Curtis knew when most people saw DHS pursuing a suspect, their thoughts always moved to a foreigner with a beard and a backpack.

"Have you seen him, ma'am?" Curtis asked after the woman studied the images for what felt like a full minute.

"No. Well, I mean yes, but he ain't here no more." She adjusted her glasses again and pulled the paper closer. "Looked like he'd been through a war, that one. Just left a few hours ago. Paid cash."

Curtis got the first confirmation that they were on the right trail. "Do you know where he went? What he may have been driving?"

"He walked out of here and turned right. South. He didn't have no car."

"Thank you, ma'am. You've been very helpful." Curtis leaned to the mic on his shoulder ready to call his men back.

"What'd he do, anyway?" the woman asked, watching the motel patrons ducking for cover outside.

"I'm sorry, ma'am. I'm not at liberty to discuss that," Curtis said, still upset he didn't even have the full details himself why John was taken into custody, or why he was pursuing him.

Curtis turned to face the window. "What room was he in?"

* * *

John's room didn't reveal any clues of his whereabouts, or what his destination could have been. It was clear by the lack of any mess that he didn't use the room for much more than catching his breath, knowing someone would eventually be on his trail.

"Nothing here, sir," one of the men said, kicking the corner of the bed with his boot. "Stone didn't leave anything behind that we could use."

"Thank you, Private."

Curtis called his men back and loaded up into the SUV. As he buckled the seatbelt and set the rifle next to him, he called Renee and Daniel. "John was here, but he left hours ago. I need you to get a location ASAP."

"Did you search his room?" Daniel asked.

"Yes. It was clean. Nothing left behind, and the sheets weren't even turned down." Curtis was annoyed at the computer tech implying he didn't know how to do his own job. "I need a destination, Daniel."

"Just head east," Renee said. *"The projections have him heading that direction already. We should have something for you before you get too far."*

"Can you be sure that he didn't find something while he was here that would have him heading in another direction?"

"We can't be certain," she said. *"All we can do is trust this program that Parker set up."*

Curtis closed his eyes at the mention of Parker's name. "Copy."

A slight twang of guilt echoed through his chest. Parker was John's friend, and Curtis felt like using the hacker's own program to track him down was a betrayal of trust. But Parker had broken the law by helping a fugitive, whether or not they thought John was innocent.

That was for the courts to decide.

"East," Curtis said to the driver, ending the call.

CHAPTER
19

Fatigue still tugged at John's limbs, his arms heavy as he kept the stolen car on the road. He was able to get a couple of hours sleep at the motel, but it was a break he couldn't afford. There was a lot of ground to cover, and any space he gave to the people trying to remove him from the picture would make his job that much harder.

He made it to New Mexico in only a couple of hours, but he had to drive another three to reach the manufacturing facility he was looking for. John parked the Toyota in the parking lot next to his target. He had stolen three cars in under three days, becoming a criminal in the process of trying to prove his innocence, though grand theft auto paled in comparison to domestic terror.

The sun was just setting as the industrial district's morning shift headed home for the night, and the evening crews arrived to start their day. *Another cold night,* John thought, as his breath puffed out in small wisps. *At least I've got a jacket this time.*

The Toyota's door thumped as he leaned in to close it, not wanting to make a loud noise. He rubbed his hands together and tucked the key into his pocket. The fuel gauge rode the edge of the *E*, but it would at least be enough to put ten or twelve miles between himself and the factory if he needed a quick escape.

The shrubs bordering the parking lot of the manufacturing facility gave John plenty of cover to maneuver around toward the rear of the building. But as he made his way along its edge, twigs tugging and poking his jacket, he saw the amount of security was far more significant than that of his first target.

Half a dozen defense contractors roamed the wide-open areas, creating overlapping fields of view covering every side of the manufacturing plant. Each man carried a submachine gun of some type, but John couldn't make out what kind from this distance in the dark. He rubbed the fingers of his empty right hand together and wiped them along the outside of his thigh, looking for the best possible approach to sneak by the guards.

The rear loading docks had plenty of regular employees wandering around. The contractors watching over them might miss John sneaking through if he could time his entrance and blend in.

He spotted an area that would be covered by only a single guard, and focused on him.

After a few minutes watching the guard's pattern, John stepped onto the asphalt and jogged toward the entrance at the corner the building, making sure to stay in the man's blind spot. He slid behind the fender of a truck, and the skidding of gravel sounded like an avalanche in John's ears. He planted himself against the vehicle and kept his eyes glued to the mercenary. The man turned away, and John seized the opening, making his way toward the door.

Crossing under two of the overhead lights, John's shadow splayed out in four different directions, rotating around like the hands on a clock. The shadow to his right elongated, and he stopped, but the movement on the ground caught the contractor's attention. The guard spun to see who was behind him. John moved in fast to close the gap. The man's eyes widened in recognition. They were expecting him.

His hand dropped to his weapon, but John pinned the SMG to the man's body. John lashed out with the web of his right between his thumb and forefinger, smashing the guard's throat.

The man's hands shot up to his neck, as he gasped for breath. John grabbed the guy's vest and pulled him close as he brought a freight train of a knee into his foe's stomach. The guard collapsed, unconscious. John worked the strap of the man's weapon free, looping it over his shoulder. He pulled the guard out of sight, just as one of the workers stepped out of a truck and spotted him.

The man saw John standing over the guard and dropped the box he carried. The cardboard carton landed on its corner and split open, spilling out its small metal contents, ringing and echoing across the complex.

"Hey!" The sound alerted a second guard, and he made his way toward the commotion with his weapon already drawn.

John crouched behind the truck, and the defense contractor snap fired two single shots. The cracks of his weapon and the sparks flying off the vehicle sent the employees scrambling away. The contractors were clearly tasked with taking John out, as a priority over the safety of the workers.

John gripped his weapon one-handed and returned fire. The UMP 45 spit a short burst, chewing up the asphalt near the aggressor. He didn't score a hit, but it was enough to force the man to move. John stepped out into the open and sprinted for the entrance, and another weapon joined the firefight from the opposite side of the building.

So much for the stealthy approach, John thought.

***

"There are reports of a firefight," Renee said. *"Not too far from your position."*

"What? Is it John?" Curtis asked.

"Unknown, but it's a strong possibility, given the data from Parker's software," Daniel said, his voice coming from the background.

"Where?"

"I'm sending the location to your vehicle's GPS now," Renee said.

The screen in the center of the vehicle's dash lit up, showing their current location, and a route to a second marker. They were only ten minutes out. Curtis started at the two dots, separated by less than twenty miles.

Is this a coincidence, or did Renee and Daniel know where they were already sending us? The thoughts gnawed at Curtis' mind, but he set it aside for the mission.

"Go," he said to the driver before looking back over his shoulder. "We've got a possible location on the target. A firefight is going on, but we don't know who's involved."

The men in the SUV traded glances and nodded to Curtis as they prepared for the hunt.

Curtis turned to face the front again. "Check your fire, watch for innocents and law enforcement. Remember, we bring John in alive."

CHAPTER 20

Dust shook and rose from the pulsing percussions emanating from the barrel of John's UMP 45. Using a nearby truck for cover, he unleashed a pair of short bursts at the contractor nearest to his position. Two bullets thudded into the man's chest, slamming into his body armor, sending him to the ground. The man fell back with a groan and rolled to the side to avoid John's follow up shots.

Only twenty feet of open ground separated John from the entrance to the building. He stepped forward, SMG against his shoulder while pressing the trigger. His rounds shattered glass and splintered wood, keeping his opponents behind cover. John held his aim as he moved, firing until the bolt locked back.

Using the brief respite from return fire, he sprinted the remaining distance to the building entrance. He gripped the door handle and yanked it open just as a contractor popped up from behind cover. Two bullets whipped by and a third struck the steel door as John made it into the building, diving in and sliding across the floor.

Inside, the employees ducked into rooms, behind crates, or fleeing as fast as they could, fearing that an armed killer just entered. A mercenary burst into the room, his weapon held low at his waist, ready to spray in wide arcs.

John hurled his empty submachine gun at the guard the moment he entered. The man was in mid-run, and the flying steel weapon caught him by total surprise. It smashed into his face and took his feet out from under him. He landed hard on the concrete floor with a smack and didn't move.

John moved toward the downed guard to take his loaded SMG. The strap pulled tight, still wrapped around the contractor's shoulder and neck. The door behind him flew open. Two mercenaries from outside leaned in on either side of the entrance, finding their target and opening fire.

Big .45 ACP rounds bit into the concrete and sparked off of the support column. John dropped to his side. Unable to take the SMG, he pulled the pistol from the man's holster, firing several shots at the opened doorway.

The two attackers ducked back, and John came up to a crouch, firing again. He held the three-dot sights steady, focusing on the front fiberoptic dot. When a target presented itself, popping out to return fire, John depressed the trigger three times in rapid succession. His first shot hit the man in the stomach, causing him to drop his arms and spoil his aim. The second round struck just above the collar, biting into the flesh of his neck. John's final shot found its mark, hitting the contractor in the head.

John dumped the rest of the pistol's magazine on the other side of the entrance to make the second merc think hard about stepping into the open. He dropped the empty handgun and found his empty UMP next to the unconscious guard. He picked up his weapon and snatched three loaded magazines from the unconscious man's chest rig.

The mercenary stepped through the doorway, weapon spitting on full-auto. John sprinted deeper into the building as more voices pierced the echo of the automatic weapon fire. He wouldn't be able to hold them all off in the middle of the loading bay. Besides John was here to find evidence, and he wouldn't get that from a bunch of dead hired guns. An empty magazine clattered to the floor as John reloaded his SMG on the run.

Thunder reverberated through the open space, rattling windows, and thumping against John's eardrums as the mercenaries gave chase. He pressed the release to chamber a round, turned, and braced himself against the frame of an open doorway. The UMP jackhammered against his shoulder, but his point of aim remained solid. His precise incoming rounds were enough to dissuade his pursuers, for now.

* * *

Curtis opened and closed his hand, working some of the cold from his extremities. The increased adrenaline pulled the blood flow closer to his core and elevated his heart rate. "How far?"

"Two minutes," the driver said.

"Weapons check," Curtis said over his shoulder.

Bolt's cycled, chambering rounds, as his team readied their M4 carbines. Curtis press checked his M9 and slid it back into the holster with the safety engaged.

"You need to get there now, Lieutenant," Renee said, impatience in her voice.

"We're one minute out," Curtis said.

He ignored Renee's follow up, thinking about why she was so concerned about them taking too long to arrive. Part of him wanted to believe that everyone at HRD was concerned not only with the innocents in the area, but also John's well being. The vibe he got from the men he shared the vehicle with spoke differently.

John, what did you get yourself into?

***

John inserted another magazine and slapped the charging handle, sending the bolt home. He shouldered the weapon and let loose with a long burst as another contractor rushed in. The bullets pounded his chest and rode up. His target fell back with a short gurgle and hiss, not wearing body armor.

More rounds punched through the drywall, shattering the windows behind John, and knocking chunks out of the desk he used for cover. Using the position of the bullet holes in the wall for reference, he returned fire with short bursts and heard two distinct voices as they shouted warnings. John ran to a second door in the office and kicked it open, rushing back into the hallway as the firing continued through the wall.

He turned and crouched, firing at a flash of movement in the entrance to the office he just left. His rounds tore at the thigh and shattered the kneecap of the man taking point. Shouts of pain caused the other mercenary to fall back. The bolt on John's UMP locked open on an empty chamber.

Turning to head down the hall, John held his empty weapon close and dipped his chin, running as fast as he could to the office entrance at the far end. He barreled into the heavy wooden door, shoulder first, and tore a chunk from the frame as it swung in. His eyes bounced around the lavish room taking in as much information as he could. John wasn't alone.

A short, thin man stood up near the oak desk, his eyes bulged in fear. Austin Pennell, the money man. A computer at his feet sparked and smoked. Several pops sent out another spray of crackling embers to the expensive carpeting.

He's destroying the data in the computer.

The man pulled the strap of a messenger bag over his head and ran out the rear exit at the far end of the spacious office. John scrambled after him. He needed either Pennell or the bag on his shoulder.

John's weapon was empty, and he didn't have time to fumble with his last magazine. He threw the door open and turned in time to see the exit to the side parking lot slamming shut. John kicked the steel crash bar and followed outside.

The cold air bit into his face and hands, but his mind was elsewhere. Sharp pistol cracks kept him focused on his quarry. Pennell tossed his bag into a Corvette and panic-fired his pistol three more times before he ducked inside. The bullets went high, as

John surged forward to eat up the remaining distance.

A mask of panic washed over the man's face, as he started the engine and saw the massive Ranger bearing down on him. The small, frightened man fired through the passenger side window, hurling pebbles of shattered glass after the bullets whizzed past. John dipped his shoulder low and struck the door, denting the panel and rocking the vehicle on its struts. The frightened driver attempted to reload his weapon as John hooked his fingers underneath, and hoisted the car up onto two wheels.

With a furious shout, he lifted two of the wheels completely off the ground. The man inside frantically dropped his pistol and fumbled, too late, to put the vehicle into gear. John gritted his teeth, his muscles tensed, and his legs drove like pistons. The car's body and frame groaned as it dropped to its side. Glass cracked, and metal creaked, as the Corvette continued to rock, threatening to completely roll upside down. It finally settled back, the door and fender crunching under its own weight.

John moved around to the other side. His quarry screamed and tugged at the belt keeping him trapped.

With a hand on the hood of the car, John braced himself and kicked the windshield with a massive boot. The frame gave way to the tremendous force and caved in enough for him to reach inside. The man inside was in a full panic now, but gunfire snapped John's attention back to the building. The two guards pursuing him through the halls emerged, firing at what little they could see of him poking out from behind the car.

John rolled toward the rear of the vehicle and grabbed his UMP still hanging by its sling. He ejected the empty magazine and retrieved the last one from his pocket, reloading the weapon. He leaned out to get a better angle and opened fire. One of the rounds from John's burst punched through the upper arm of the lead man, forcing him to release his grip on his gun.

The second man shouted and walked forward dumping his entire mag at the car John was leaning against. Plastic cracked, and metal rang out, protesting from the assault. He heard a sudden whoosh and felt an intense heat emanating from the rear of the car. Gunfire had punctured the fuel tank and ignited the gas flowing out.

John pushed off the car and sprinted away. His boots tore up chunks of gravel with each step, and the gunfire continued from behind him. A ball of fire erupted, engulfing the rear half of the Corvette. The man trapped inside screamed in agony and terror.

Flames crept forward, devouring the seats, the leather interior, and the clothes of the driver.

The bag inside!

John's focus locked onto the front seat where the messenger bag full of files hung, hooked on the seatbelt catch. The material started browning as the strap itself warped and melted before igniting. He ran forward, but the automatic weapon fire from the other contractor stopped him short as he skidded and fell back. Raising his SMG John fired a quick burst and rolled behind a steel drum trash can.

Sparks shot out, as his assailant punched holes into the drum. John's instincts kicked into overdrive. He settled into an eerie calm, tracking the rhythm of the shooting. The mercenary used a steady technique, triggering a series of short bursts in the same beat.

Finally, in a brief moment of calm, John heard the clatter of a plastic object hit the ground. Pivoting out from behind cover, John came up into a crouch, weapon braced against his body. He locked his front sight onto the man, now stepping past the car on its side, and depressed the trigger. A quick two-round burst caught the man in the torso, folding him over just enough to disrupt his reloading.

John stood and pressed forward, firing two more quick bursts before holding the trigger to empty the magazine at near point blank range. Three of the rounds punched through the soft body armor, but the ones that didn't, caused enough blunt force trauma to seriously injure and incapacitate the mercenary.

Smoke poured from the broken front windshield of the overturned car, and the driver had long stopped his screaming. John reached inside to pull the messenger bag out, before tossing it to the ground and stomping out the flames that threatened to swallow every last shred of evidence he fought to retrieve.

Sirens in the distance bled through the crackling flames consuming the car. John scooped the remains of the bag up, and peered inside, seeing that not everything was burnt to a crisp. He tucked it under his arm and ran for a row of vans and trucks with the manufacturing facility's logo on the side.

Most didn't appear to have any keys inside, but the two on the far end, both trucks, had a key dangling from the ignition. John pulled the door open and slipped inside, tossing the burnt bag into the passenger seat.

* * *

The SUV's brakes chattered, bringing the speeding vehicle to a stop. Curtis already had the door opened, and stepped out with his M4 carbine held at a low ready.

"On me."

The other three team members exited and moved into position. Gunfire on the other side of the building echoed out as a series of bursts, with some metal ringing in the distance. The team moved to the corner and sliced around it. They reached the other side of the property, then heard the sound of sustained automatic fire.

Out of instinct, Curtis and the other members of his team pressed their bodies closer to the building and dropped to a combat crouch. The firing stopped, and Curtis waited for an internal three-count before giving the signal to continue moving forward. As they stepped around to the other parking lot, all four men stopped in their tracks, not expecting the scene that greeted them.

The only sounds were the crackling of the fire engulfing a car turned on its side, and the distant wail of approaching sirens. Curtis, awestruck by the devastation, stepped out into the open. One man, wearing military-style gear, lay on the floor bleeding from a wound in his upper arm.

"Check him," Curtis said. "Get that wound treated."

One of the men let his rifle hang from its sling, and pulled out a small trauma kit. Curtis stepped around the vehicle, looking it up and down and inspecting the bullet holes all along its underside. Around the front of the car, or top, really, he saw the remains of someone in the driver's seat. The front windshield had been smashed in, probably while the vehicle rested on its side.

Curtis brought his weapon to his shoulder when spotted another man on the ground, wearing similar gear to the injured man. He scanned the area taking short steps, as his boots scattered spent shell casings.

This looks like John's work, he thought.

An engine growled to life, and Curtis dropped to one knee, bringing his M4 up. The rest of his team moved up rifles at the ready. A white pickup truck rolled out into the open, heading for them. The driver stopped, and the glare from the overhead lights wiped across the windshield. Curtis was staring at John Stone sitting behind the wheel.

He held his aim low, at the hood of the vehicle, but still close enough in case he needed to fire. "It's over, John," he called out.

John shook his head slowly. "It's a setup, Clarke."

Curtis couldn't hear the words with the truck's window up, but John mouthed the words clear enough.

"Let me bring you in. We can clear this—"

Gunfire erupted to Curtis' right. John ducked a split-second before the firing as the bullets cracked the windshield.

"He's got a gun!" one of his own teammates yelled before shooting again.

Chaos swirled, as the others joined the shooting. Curtis stood, shouting for them to hold their fire. The truck lurched and backed away, sparks lighting up the entire front of it. The rear bumper took out a fence post before the truck spun around and drove off. John slammed into a fence at the rear of the property, before disappearing over a hill.

"I said hold your fire!" Curtis waved his arms and shouted as the last shot went off.

"He was reaching, LT. I saw it," the first shooter said.

Curtis let his weapon hang and clutched his head with both hands as the sirens approached. He and his men were here on an official government operation, but he knew that the police would arrive, ready to trade fire with anyone and everyone involved in the firefights that occurred here. It was going to be a dicey situation, and he needed to get his men back in line. *Back on their leashes.*

CHAPTER
21

Smoke poured from the grill and out from the numerous bullet holes in the hood of the truck. John parked it off to the side of the road, as far away as he could, from the busy street. The engine sputtered and died before he even had to turn the key. The burnt bag filled the cabin with the aroma of an inviting campfire.

John looked down at the submachine gun hanging on his shoulder. The bolt was locked open, a stark reminder that the weapon had run dry in the last encounter. He resisted the urge to wipe his prints off of it, rubbing a thumb along the grip. *Not like they won't know that I was the one that carried it.*

He grabbed the bag and left the empty UMP in the driver seat, stripping the bolt from the weapon, to toss away in a trash can. John stepped out into the cold, and the temperature change was a physical barrier, almost pushing him back in the dead truck. A gust of wind whipped through and slipped into one sleeve and under the collar of his jacket. The light material didn't do much to stave of the chill, and the air that made it through brought a level of discomfort bordering on pain.

John zipped the messenger bag against his ribs under the jacket and tucked his hands underneath his arms. He ducked behind the low collar of the jacket as best he could, walking into the dark night as the first flakes of an evening snowfall started.

John stayed out of the light as much as possible, putting distance between himself and the truck. He blew into his hands, rubbing them together as he jogged across a dark street, heading toward a faint flickering orange glow. A fire of some kind. The last thing he needed was to interact with people while he was on the run, but with the cold seeping deep into his bones, and his teeth starting to chatter, John was drawn to the distant flame like a moth.

He stayed deep in the shadows while approaching. The area he wandered into was run down, mostly empty, and best of all, dark, except for the fire burning inside a beat up old steel drum. Several people were standing near the flickering orange beast with another group on the out edges of the glow, talking and drinking.

He pulled his hat lower and clutched his jacket closed as he walked up. As soon as he stepped into the outer edge of the fire's glow, John held his hands out, just below shoulder height to show he meant the group no harm. A few of the people in the group seemed a bit alarmed at a stranger approaching, but the oldest looking man of the group greeted him with a warm and inviting smile.

"Welcome, friend," the man said, looking down at John's clothing. "Name's Henry."

"Evening," John replied taking stock of the man.

Henry stood taller than the rest of his group, or at least the ones near the fire. His dark, weathered skin was a stark contrast to his white beard and hair. He wore an old, worn out olive drab coat. Even in the dark, the collar, style of pockets and the fit were familiar to John.

"You got a name, friend?" Henry asked as he covered the remaining distance and offered his hand.

John shook the offered hand and gave him a wary smile. "Safer not to say. But you can call me Frank."

Henry looked him up and down again with an inquisitive grin. "Whatever you say, Frank."

"Army?" Frank asked, nodding at Henry's jacket.

He tugged at one of the collars and brushed down one side. "Eight years," Henry said. "Just doing my part to make sure the Commies didn't storm our shores."

John just smiled and nodded.

"Of course, when the Cold War ended I got out." Henry scratched through his beard along the side of his jaw with a finger. "Not too long before Desert Storm, so we didn't have our shining moment either. And that's how it felt when we got home. No special treatment, no help to settle into civilian life. Just a bunch of people looking right through us, as if we weren't even there."

"I get that. Like as long as they're safe, people don't notice the soldiers getting up before dawn every morning to get the job done." John rubbed his hands and held them over the fire.

Henry stared out into the distance nodding. "What about you, Frank? Did you serve?"

John thought for a moment about the possible answers he could give. He could see in Henry's eyes he suspected already. "Rangers," he said, almost too low to be heard.

Henry's eyebrows raised a bit. "Lead the way, huh?"

John crossed his arms, staring into the dancing flames. "Doesn't feel so much like that nowadays."

"I don't blame you. Got a Navy gal back there that knows what it's like too." Henry nodded a head back to the rest of the people huddled at the edge of the glow eating and talking.

"Seems society isn't getting any better lately," John said, more to himself than to Henry.

"Can't be mad at the people. They're not the ones that put us here." Henry looked around at the others and scratched the side of his nose. "Not really mad at the government either, if I'm being honest."

John followed Henry's gaze and nodded in understanding.

"I don't know what your situation is, Frank, but I still see the fire in you. You'll get back on your feet." He shot a thumb over his shoulder. "These men and women behind me are young, and they got that same look in your eye. There's hope for all of them, still."

* * *

Curtis watched the police gathering evidence at the truck John abandoned, wisps of smoke still rising from the perforated hood. He pressed the web of his hands between thumbs and forefingers together, more out of a nervous habit than the need to actually adjust the fit of his gloves. The sun had come up an hour earlier, but it was still too cold for the light layer of snow covering everything to melt.

After the firefight, John fled late the night before, Curtis stuck around to wait for the police. He couldn't follow John without the cops chasing all of them. There was no telling how his team would respond to law enforcement intervening if they caught up to John.

The Lieutenant stayed up while the rest of his team found a place to get some sleep so they could continue the pursuit. The way his team reacted was very disconcerting. John had both hands visible, talking to him when one of his own men opened fire.

All three agreed that they saw John reaching for something, but Curtis was still unconvinced. He was looking John in the eye as he spoke and had a clear mental image of John's hands tightening on the steering wheel. Either way, he needed answers, and finding John, without having to worry about another violent encounter, was paramount.

Leaving the scene behind, Curtis needed to find the most likely direction that someone would take, hoping to avoid detection after abandoning a vehicle here. He pulled the zipper higher under his chin and pulled his collar up. John wouldn't be able to make it too far in this weather. He would have had to find shelter somewhere.

Curtis ducked into the entrance of a small hardware store not yet open. He peeled one of his gloves off and scrolled through his contacts to make a call, facing away from the daggers of chilled air.

"Miranda. Is Renee there?" He put a finger to his other ear. "No, that's fine. Better, really. I need your help, but let's try to keep this between us. I'm not so sure I can trust the oversight team right now."

He filled Dr. Spencer in on the details of his run-in with John, and the team opening fire. They discussed possible methods to track John without the others knowing, but the best she could do was pass Curtis the latest data from Parker's mob recognition program. It didn't pinpoint John, but at least he had a direction now.

After an hour of walking, he reached a point where the possible paths diverged. Curtis readjusted his sunglasses and took a long hard look down each choice before deciding on the direction that led him through the rougher terrain. The tracking software had nothing beyond this point, so it was all gut instinct from here on.

He reached a bit of a clearing out of the way of most people, where a group of homeless men and women had set up a small camp. There were plenty of small makeshift tents, but none looked really suitable for the brutal winter moving in. Most of the people were still inside trying to get some sleep, a few fidgeting and struggling to stay warm. An older man watched Curtis approach and stepped out to greet him.

The man had gray and white hair, including his thick beard. He wore an apprehensive smile, trying to stay friendly. Curtis realized that he still wore his dark HRD uniform, with a pistol holstered on his hip. He removed his sunglasses, tucking them into an unused loop on his vest, and lifted his hat and settled it down a little higher, hoping to appear far less threatening.

"Morning," he said, keeping his hands up and away from the firearm.

The older man nodded his head. "Can I help you?"

"I'm hoping so," Curtis said. "I'm Lieutenant Clarke, and I just need to know if you've seen someone that we're looking for."

"We? You with the police or the feds?"

Curtis smiled. "Uh, feds, officially." He held his hand out. "What's your name?"

The man paused, looking down at the offered hand as Curtis covered the remaining distance. Finally, he accepted the greeting and shook hands. "Name's Henry." The questioning smile faded replaced with concern and confusion.

"Pleasure," Curtis said. He reached into his back pocket slowly to avoid alarming anyone and pulled out a folded printout. Curtis unfolded the page with a printed image, also wrapped around a smaller photograph. He handed the sheet of paper to Henry.

"Have you seen this man around last night, or any time this morning?"

Henry looked down at the image, a printout from security camera footage in a dark office, with the face highlighted. The old man pressed his lips together and slowly shook his head. "Can't say I have."

Curtis handed him the photo, John's picture used for his HRD identification badge. He paid close attention to the expression and the way it changed when Henry looked at the better quality image. He recognized John and judging by the shifting eyes, and small twitches, he had a close interaction.

"His name is John Stone. He's a fugitive, and considered extremely dangerous."

Henry looked up at Curtis, handing the pieces of paper back, his small, accommodating smile returning.

"Is he here now? If he is, you can tell me. I can help you. I can help him."

"Sorry, Lieutenant. I haven't seen this man before." He folded his arms across his chest, partly due to the cold, but the gesture felt more defiant.

Curtis knew, then, that John was here, but had most likely already moved on. The men and women here weren't going to be of much assistance, and he didn't want to cause any more trouble for them than they already faced with the weather shifting.

He tugged the brim of his hat back down and put his sunglasses on. "Well, thank you for your help, Henry." Curtis slipped the pages back into his pocket and pulled out his wallet, taking out the few bills inside. It wasn't much, but he felt the need to offer something. Was it guilt? Pity? He didn't know, but right now that wasn't important.

"It's not much, but maybe you can get some hot coffee, or soup for everyone here," Curtis said, handing over the cash.

Henry looked down at the offered bills and scratched his ear before accepting it, pride taking a back seat to necessity. "Thank you, Clarke, was it?"

"Yes, sir."

"Thank you, Lieutenant Clarke," Henry said, tucking the money into a pocket. "And if you find your man, John, I truly hope you're able to help him out."

CHAPTER
22

John had fallen asleep for a couple of hours with Henry and the others, but it was time he could ill afford to lose. Just as the sun poked up over the buildings in the distance, he left them behind, hoping to avoid being seen with the group and keeping them out of trouble.

Before he left, John spent a few minutes shuffling through what was left of the paperwork inside the messenger bag. Most of the pages were burnt in the fire, but several of the sheets were folded and tucked along the far edge. John compared the information on everything he found with the notes he obtained from his previous internet search, and the files he found from the interior design firm.

The unburnt pages didn't contain much more information than he already had, but bits of the other pages helped him connect a prominent dot with other operations he was looking into before. It was a name he recognized, Monte Buchanan. He initially thought nothing of it, lumping Buchanan in with other rich and powerful people that John figured were just funding the operations.

What he had hoped for was the name at the top. The man pulling strings in the whole operation. The one that wanted him out of the picture for getting too close, after taking Warren Ratcliffe out and securing the Guardian. Perhaps Monte could fill in that blank.

Discovering the next location he needed to get to, John dumped the messenger bag into the barrel to feed the fire as he departed. What concerned him more was how Curtis found out where he would be last night. The men he brought weren't familiar, but the way they opened fire told John that they were more likely part of the group sent in to oversee the hostile response division operations. There was a good chance that those men were loyal to the man John was after. Did that mean Lieutenant Clarke had turned as well?

His breath was visible, as he blew into his ungloved hands and ducked underneath a board blocking the entrance to an abandoned building. Time. That's what he needed now, but it was in such short supply. Dust motes swirled around in the shafts of golden morning light poking through the broken windows and rotted boards. The air smelled stale, still cold, but without the wind lancing through to John's muscles. It was a good enough place to gather his thoughts.

"How did you find me, Clarke?" John's voice was a commanding presence in the empty building, even though he spoke softly. He already knew the answer, though his mind tried to deny it.

"Parker."

The pieces started falling into place. Parker was helping them, using his *mob recognition* program. From what he remembered, the program used a person's physical attributes and the way they moved, matching those of known associates. It gave him the ability to find people with a high degree of accuracy, without requiring facial recognition, even in a crowd.

John didn't think it was as accurate for hunting individuals, but Parker was a capable computer wizard, with a knack for bending machines to his will. What was necessary now was to try and avoid the system. His physical attributes, like height and weight, were set. But the way he moved, his posture and gait, could be altered to fool the mob recognition software.

The golden glow faded as the light took on more of a yellowish white. Late morning. John had to get back out there, and head to the next location. Frozen limbs and joints protested as he rose and stepped back out into the icy winds. He stuffed his hands into his pockets and hunched his shoulders, taking smaller steps at more of a hurried pace. Enough to alter his usual movement. *I hope it's enough.*

* * *

"I'm almost positive John was here," Curtis said, holding his hands up to the warm air blowing out of the SUV's vents. "I need you to focus the mob recognition search starting from my current location. And let's try to keep the wonder twins out of this if you can."

"That might be a little tough."

Curtis rubbed his hands together. "They're in the computer lab now, aren't they?"

"Yes. Renee is looking at the latest data," Miranda said.

Not knowing who was involved in what he now felt was a setup, Curtis didn't know if he could trust Renee and Daniel. He had hoped to get more information about John's possible whereabouts, but if the HRD leadership had all of the same information, he would still be deployed with the men that opened fire during their last mission.

"Alright. Just do what you need to do, even if you've got to let Renee and Daniel know, Doctor."

"Of course. I'll call you with any updated information."

"Thank you." Curtis put his phone away and opened up his small laptop in the vehicle. The latest reports, and other notes provided by his support team, including Dr. Spencer, Renee, and Daniel, were sent to a directory specific to him. He spent a minute organizing the newest data and tried to figure out John's movements.

The rest of his team entered the vehicle, securing their gear. Curtis put his computer away and buckled his seatbelt. The driver slid into the seat and shifted into reverse, backing out of the parking lot.

"Where to, sir?" he asked.

Curtis took in a breath and let it out through his nose. "HRD rally point three."

With no further data, all Curtis could do was to direct his team to a small government building, tasked with assisting them in the hunt for John. It provided no significant advantage, but he didn't want to be out on the road, heading in the wrong direction for an entire day once Miranda's new search provided any potentially usable intel. His best tactic would be to sit tight and wait for more information. The rally point was a couple of hours from their location, which gave Curtis some time to catch up on some much-needed sleep.

He pulled his hat low over his eyes. "Wake me when we're close, or if anything important comes up."

CHAPTER 23

Miranda sent Curtis the full results of her latest search, using the starting point and possible direction she received. He wouldn't see it until his team reached the next rally point in half an hour. But when he got a chance to read it, she knew it wouldn't be the results he hoped for. Unlike all of their other runs with the mob recognition software, she had found absolutely no trace of John.

They had been able to track him up to that point with the widely spaced waypoints in the rare moments when the software had been able to find him. Parker's mob recognition used the new data to go back over older footage and build a more reliable pattern to extrapolate a possible direction and focus more attention on those updated parameters.

This time, however, not a single trace of John had been returned. Even feeding data from previous searches into the new search yielded nothing usable.

It was like he went to ground, no longer on the move. All trace of their quarry had vanished.

Miranda argued with Daniel as he accused her of fouling the parameters to make sure the program wouldn't work. Renee believed her, knowing that Miranda didn't have enough experience with Parker's quirky software to do that without it being apparent to them.

She left the computer lab after sending the results to Curtis, but her subconscious led her through the HRD facility while her mind ran through different ways to help John. She knew the answer, and by the time Miranda admitted it to herself what it was, she already reached the holding cells where they were keeping Parker. If anyone knew how to find John, it would be him.

The guard watching the cells reluctantly let Miranda by to talk to Parker, but he wasn't going to let him out so she would have to be careful what she said. The MP escorted her to a cell near the far end, and she noted that all of the others were empty. The man nodded his head toward Parker's cell and stopped a few feet short as she walked over. He stayed within earshot but stayed back far enough to almost feel as if he gave them a bit of privacy.

Parker leaned to one side, peeking around the corner to see his visitors. His eyes lit up when he saw

Miranda. "Doctor Spencer." He did his best to keep the emotion in his eyes from reaching his mouth as he spoke.

"Parker. How are you doing in here?" She approached the door and glanced back at the guard before getting too close to the bars.

Parker's eyes kept darting back and forth between the guard and Miranda. "I'm okay. How about John? What have they done with him?"

She pressed her lips together, not wanting to get Parker's hopes up too high. "He escaped." Miranda looked down at his feet. "With your help."

Parker stepped forward and grabbed the bars, his eyes widened. "Where is he now?"

"We don't know. That's why I'm here, Parker. I need your help to find him."

"Where's Van Pierce? Is he still relieved of command?"

Miranda looked up at him again. "Yes. He's confined to his quarters."

"And Curtis? Is he in his quarters too?"

A small hint of a smile tugged at the corner of Dr. Spencer's mouth. "No. He's out looking for John. That's why I need your help," Miranda said.

"How? Are they releasing me?" Parker asked, smiling.

"The mob recognition. They're using it to track John."

Parker's face drained of color. His eyes dropped. "How did they figure it out so fast?"

"I'm helping them," Miranda said, sadness in her eyes.

"Why? Why would you help the people framing John?" Parker's knuckles whitened.

"Stay calm, prisoner," the guard said.

Miranda closed her eyes and drooped her head forward. "Curtis needs to be the one to bring John in. Alive. To do that, he needs all the help he can get."

"Why can't you two just help John find out who is behind the setup?" Parker asked. "Uncover the people above Warren Ratcliffe, and maybe we can clear John's name."

"They would lock us both up as well," Miranda stepped closer, grabbing the bars just above Parker's hands. "The men after John are treating him like a terrorist threat and shooting first."

"Step back, Doctor," the guard said as he approached.

Parker's eyes welled up as he stared at Miranda "What?"

"If Curtis doesn't find him before the new command's teams do, they will kill him."

The guard wrapped a hand around Miranda's upper arm. "I said step back from the cell." He tugged her back as she tried to resist.

"Okay," Parker said.

Miranda let go of the bars and held her hands up, taking one step back. It was enough to appease the MP.

"I'll help you," Parker said.

"Thank you." Miranda took the notepad and pen from her pocket as Parker explained how she could modify the program.

* * *

"Thank you," John said, closing the door of the pickup truck with a metallic thud.

"No, thank you," the driver said. "For your service."

John nodded as the man drove away, his truck belching a gray and white plume behind it as it rumbled off into the distance. John had hitchhiked his way across two more states to reach South Dakota. He was at the proverbial doorstep of his destination, but the weather here was much colder than New Mexico. He still only wore the light jacket, but the man in the truck had given John a pair of old mittens. They smelled of cigarette smoke and beef jerky, and they would be of no use in a firefight. It was nice to have warm fingers until then, however.

He pulled the zipper up higher and jogged out of the wind and snow flurries. John approached the upscale neighborhood as the last of the sun's light faded. He had endured the colder climate and approached his target destination at night when the temperature dropped. Knowing he would have stood out in broad daylight, it was his only choice.

Walking the entire perimeter would look too suspicious, so John headed along the sidewalk running in front of the vast plot of land, turning the corner to walk down the west side of the mansion. He could see at least two men guarding the entrances. One in front and one on the side.

That meant there were most likely another in the back, and one on the east side of the home. They all wore suits with thick overcoats and gloves, but none carried any visible weapons. Each also had secret service style earpieces tucked under their collars. *Highly paid private security,* John thought, making a note of the expensive clothing.

With no weapons of his own and no clear sign of what he would be looking for, John would have to act quickly once he made it inside. With the limited information, he figured an approach on the east side would be the most advantageous. It didn't face the street, like the front and west side, which gave him more shadows to use for his approach. John had no reason to assume that the east end would have more than one man as well.

He continued walking around the block, looping back until he reached the field connecting to the mansion's spacious yard. John kept his eyes moving, looking for anyone watching him as he veered into the shadows. Leaning against a tree, John took off his bulky mittens. The warmth they provided was enjoyable, but he would need full manual dexterity to maneuver.

He spent a moment contemplating trying to stuff them into his jacket's pockets but ultimately decided to ditch them by the tree. If he absolutely needed them, he could always double back and pick them up again.

Not even a full minute had passed, and John already missed the soothing comfort as he rubbed his hands together to fight off the needles whipping through the wind. He controlled his breath to avoid puffing out visible vapors, as he approached the lights along the outer perimeter of the mansion's boundaries. His gut instinct was correct. Only one man watched this side of the house.

John watched as the sentry turned to walk the other direction, patrolling his zone. With the way clear, John jumped up and hoisted himself up onto the concrete pillar that the sturdy gate was bolted to. His boots pounded into the hard, icy grass with a thud, but the cold had stiffened his joints making the landing much harder than he would have liked.

Knees still aching, John moved into a pool of shadows from the only tree on this side of the property. He glanced out and watched the man guarding the building. In the distance, John saw a faint red glow at the side entrance. A security panel, most likely controlling a magnetic lock on the door. He squinted, watching the guard turn. He had hoped to see a hint or sign that the man carried the card necessary to access the door, but the bulky clothing meant John would have to take the hands-on approach to find out. *Wonderful.*

John stuck to the outer edge of the lawn, circling as far as he could before stepping into the line of sight of the guard patrolling the back of the house. As soon as the sentry turned and made his way toward the front, John ignored the stiffness in his legs and kept low, as he cut the distance between them in half. He slowed down, doing his best to keep the noise of his boots crunching the frozen ground. John's vision narrowed and he clenched his jaw tighter, approaching his target.

Time slowed as the sentry turned, sensing something wrong. This guy was good. John made sure his shadow or the sound of his boots on the ground didn't give away his approach, but the man's instinct alerted him to danger.

The sentry's eyes brightened, and his mouth dropped open. Something told him there was a danger to the rear, but his brain wasn't ready to face the actual threat. John stole the moment to lunge in fast, thrusting his forearm into the man's throat before he could vocalize that there was an intruder. He tackled the thinner man onto the hard packed ground and slammed an elbow into his jaw, knocking him unconscious. Clouds of condensation puffed from John's mouth as he sucked in ragged breaths. He groaned as he got to his feet and hooked his hands under each one of the sentry's arms, dragging him closer to the building, into the shadows.

The man wouldn't be out cold for much longer, but he had a couple of sets of flexible cuffs, making John's life a little easier. John bound the guard's hands and feet, gagging him with his own handkerchief and necktie. He took the guard's thick overcoat and slipped it on, enjoying the comforting warmth. He opted to leave the gloves behind but dug through the man's pockets until he found the key card inside a wallet.

John slipped the HK VP40 pistol from the man's shoulder rig along with the spare magazine, that had another thirteen rounds of .40 caliber. He pinched the card between his lips and dropped the extra mag into his pocket. With the pistol in hand, John held the keycard to the small panel, and the light flashed green as an audible click unlocked the door.

CHAPTER
24

Curtis strode down the hall, his boots thumping with each impatient step. He reached the lab and poked his head in the door. Renee and Daniel were huddled over one of the displays, pointing at the data scrolling in, and whispering their thoughts. Neither looked like they got any sleep. Curtis could relate. He had hardly been able to close his eyes either.

He looked around the room and spotted Dr. Spencer curled up on one of the chairs, wrapped in a stiff, olive drab blanket. She adjusted and opened her eyes as his footsteps echoed in the mostly quiet room. Renee glanced back, but Daniel never took his eyes off of the screen.

"Do you guys have anything for me?" Curtis asked.

"Not yet," Renee said.

"Nothing? It's been almost two days."

"Stone's a ghost," Daniel said. "He just disappeared after he left the homeless camp."

"I don't understand, how could be that hard to find." Curtis turned to Miranda. "Didn't Parker give you anything to help out?"

"He did." Miranda put her glasses on and slipped her shoes onto her feet, staying wrapped in the blanket. "We upgraded all of the algorithms and made the modifications to the code itself, but now there's so much more data to process."

Curtis furrowed his brow. "Is Parker still trying to help John by flooding our system with garbage?"

"It doesn't appear that way," Daniel said. "The stuff coming in looks promising, but even with this entire room churning through it, there's just not much we can do but wait."

"Parker wants us to find John. He wants you to find him, Lieutenant," Miranda said. "It's the only chance we have of bringing him in alive."

"I can't do that if we don't have any actionable—"

Daniel bolted upright in his chair. "Got something," he said, fingers flying over the keys.

Curtis rushed over and stood behind the computer techs. "What is it?"

"It's small, but it was enough for Parker's mods to pick out." Daniel brought up a window and scrubbed through the footage, stopping at the timestamp in the report he received.

In the image, John walked by the frame. His face was obscured by the angle and his jacket's collar, but the stride was unmistakable.

"Why is it only flagging such a small part of the feed?" Daniel mumbled as he brought up more footage from the same security system.

"Where is that footage coming from?" Curtis asked.

Daniel ignored him as a second window popped up, showing a man walking across the frame. The tech matched the timestamps from the two camera feeds and played it at normal speed. The man in the video walked across the screen before appearing on both screens where the cameras overlapped. "Why is it only flagging such a small part?"

"Did Parker's changes screw everything up?" Renee's voice was thick with frustration, bordering on anger.

"I think he's still trying to help him escape," Curtis said, leaning in closer.

"No." Miranda adjusted her glasses and wedged between Curtis and Renee.

"What is it, Doctor?" Curtis asked, giving her more room.

She stared at the footage again. "Can you rewind it, Daniel?" There was something that caught her attention. It was subtle, but from further back, the shift was a little easier to spot.

"John knows," Miranda said.

"What does he know?" Daniel asked, adjusting his own glasses.

Miranda stepped back and draped the blanket across the back of an empty chair. "He knows we're using the mob recognition to track him."

"How do you know that?" Renee asked.

"He's changing his posture and stride," Curtis said as he watched the footage again. "The program flagged him because, for this small instance, he slipped. Went back to his old movement patterns."

"It was just enough for the new program to pick out," Miranda said.

"Where is this footage from?" Curtis asked again.

***

Music greeted John at the end of a long hallway, along with the faintest smell of a cigar wafting through the air. He wanted to look for any clues in Monte Buchanan's office before engaging, but plans change. It was the nature of the beast.

With the pistol held at low ready, John crept down the long hall. He controlled his footfalls to reduce the sounds of his boots on the polished hardwood floors. As he passed each doorway, he peered through aiming his pistol to cover any potential threats. At the end of the hallway, John stepped into Monte's study. A room so lavishly decorated, it could undoubtedly appear in any number of catalogs selling high-end decorative furnishings.

Monte Buchanan sat back in a plush leather chair, facing the fireplace and watching a TV mounted above the mantle. A cloud of cigar smoke swirled above his head, spreading out as it rose. He placed a glass on the small table at his side, probably some ridiculously expensive single malt scotch, and noticed John standing at his flank, pistol in hand.

"What's the problem?" Monte asked before his brain processed the scene.

The coat John wore, and the pistol he held made Monte think he was one of the guards at first. The instant the truth hit him, he scrambled away, falling from his chair.

"Don't," John said, grasping the gun firmly in one hand, pointing it at his target's chest. "If you alert anyone or reach for a weapon, you won't like what happens next."

"What do you want from me?" Monte held his hands up in front of his face, cowering behind the small flesh and bone shields.

"I want information." John stepped closer and nudged the man in his slippered foot with a boot. "Get up. I need you to connect a few dots for me."

"Dots? I-I don't know anything." Monte crawled away on all fours, looking over his shoulder as he moved toward one of the far corners.

John swept the overcoat open wider and crouched next to the cowering man and letting his pistol dangle down pointing to the ground. "I think you know a lot more than you're letting on, Buchanan. I just need you to start spilling your guts, figuratively, before I make you spill them literally." He tapped the man's leg with the side of his pistol.

A puddle spread out from around the man's legs. His pupils opened up, almost swallowing the entire hazel irises around them.

CHAPTER
25

"I need to hitch a ride now, brother." Curtis held the phone to his ear as he made his way to grab his gear. "I know what time it is, but this can't wait. I need to get to South Dakota yesterday."

He held the phone up to his ear with a shoulder and prepped his plate carrier. "Just get me to the nearest airstrip, I'll take care of the rest."

Curtis slipped the phone back into his pocket and dropped his gear into a duffel bag, hoisting it up onto one shoulder and stepping back out into the hall.

"Lieutenant, where are you going?" Daniel asked, clutching a binder under one arm and cradling a pair of styrofoam cups of coffee in his free hand.

"You saw what doctor Spencer found, I'm on my way to John's last known position. He can't get too far before I get there."

"He knows we're tracking him. If John is as capable as you think he is, he's already out of the state."

Curtis adjusted the strap of his bag, settling it higher on his shoulder. "It's the only confirmation of his location we've had in days. When you and Renee get a lock on John, I'll need you to guide me the rest of the way."

Daniel stuck the tip of his tongue out, pressing his lips closed as he tried to think of something to say. "What about your team?"

With a *whump* Curtis' bag hit the floor. "Daniel, I really don't know where you stand on this whole ordeal, but I'm not sure if I can trust the men that were with me when we crossed paths with John the first time."

"What happened?" Daniel's brows furrowed, genuine curiosity on his face.

"I put it in my report," Curtis said. "The three men with me opened fire without provocation when we spotted John."

Daniel's posture straightened. "I read all the after action reports." He pressed his elbow tighter against the files under his arm and grabbed one of the coffee cups from his other hand. "Every man corroborated the first man's assessment. They all said John reached for something."

"His hands were on the wheel the entire time. Didn't you read my report?"

Daniel looked Curtis in the eye. "Lieutenant, your report said the same as the others."

***

Buchanan curled up into the corner as far as he could, willing himself to sink into the baseboard. He held up his hands in a futile attempt to ward the intruder away.

"P-Pryce," he said, lips quivering. "His name is Pryce Windham."

John crouched in front of the frightened man. "Windham is the one calling all the shots? The one that was giving orders to Warren Ratcliffe?"

Monte nodded his head vigorously, his voice failing him.

With the still cold barrel of the unfired pistol, John nudged the man's right hand. "I'm not sure I can trust your answer. I didn't even get to break any of your fingers."

"It's Windham, I swear." Tears streamed down his face, dribbling onto his expensive smoking jacket. "Just don't kill me."

A playful grin crept across John's face. An expression of pure amusement moving up into his eyes. "Oh, I can't do that yet. All I've got is a name. You still haven't told me where to find Mr. Windham."

John hoisted Monte onto his feet leaving one of his slippers in the corner as he dragged him down the hall toward the office.

John sat him down in front of the computer. "Get me what I need, and I'll get out of your hair. At least what's left of it."

Hands shaking and fighting back sobs, Monte navigated through the files on his desktop, printing out any and all relevant information on John's next target.

"Pryce is going to kill me. Please, you have to help."

"First of all, I already plan on paying Mr. Windham a visit and airing my grievances face to face." John pulled the fat man out of his chair. He was going to find as much info as he could about Windham before he left.

"Second, after I talk to him, he'll be in no condition to take action against anyone that helped me track him down."

Monte seemed to relax at that until John latched onto the back of the man's neck with a vise-like grip.

"Third, what makes you think *I* won't kill you when I'm done?"

Buchanan's eyes were saucers, wet with tears and reflecting the overhead light. John smiled and gave him a hard slap on the back, knocking him forward again.

"Relax, Monte, you'll live to see—"

A sharp beep in the distance cut him off as one of the outside doors opened. Two sets of footsteps echoed through the hardwood hallway.

"Mr. Buchanan, are you in trouble?" The voice was firm, with a calm and professional tone.

John held a finger to his lips.

The men came in from the same door John had used. They found the guard he tied up. He kept his left hand on the back of Monte's neck and held the VP40 in his right.

Glancing over his shoulder, John looked at the window leading out to the backyard. The sill was just below chest height, but given that the two men hunting for him were approaching and clearing the house cautiously, he had enough time to slide it open and slip out—

"He's got a gun!" Monte shouted.

Footsteps sounded in the hall, and Buchanan made a break for the door, taking advantage of John's lapse in attention. John shoved his boot into the fat man's back, sending him airborne through the doorway. Monte crashed against the hallway wall with a yelp and nearly bounced back into the room.

John seized the opportunity caused by the distraction and bolted toward the window. He fired three shots to weaken the bullet-resistant glass and dove against it with his forearms over his head.

The impact with the glass jarred his entire body. He thought for a split second that the window would stop him from escaping the house. But the glass gave way, and he tumbled out into the yard.

John hit the ground hard, and the air escaped his lungs, and the pages Buchanan just printed, scattered around him. John reached out to grab as many as he could when he heard a guard inside approaching the broken window. He turned and headed back into the cold, as the sentry called to radio for backup.

Forced to leave some of the pages behind, John patted at the coat and felt several sheets still in the breast pocket. Wind whipped icy flakes into whirling patterns, as the snowfall increased in intensity. He used the weather and the darkness to cover his escape, climbing back over the wall to flee. No need to stand and fight when he finally had the name of the man he was looking for. Pryce Windham.

CHAPTER
26

Curtis pulled the strap of the bag across his body, feeling the weight of the plate carrier and M4 inside. He waved to the pilot and walked along the tarmac toward the black GMC Yukon that Daniel helped him acquire. He checked his phone for the latest updates on the search for John when a new message popped up.

He stopped at the rear bumper of the vehicle and stared down, making sure he read the message right. Dumping the bag into the back of the SUV, Curtis called Miranda.

As the engine rumbled awake, the call connected to the speakers inside. "You there, Doctor?"

"Yes. Are you on the way to John's last known position?"

"I just landed, I'm about half an hour away," Curtis said.

"You might want to hurry," Miranda said.

Curtis looked at the information console as if Dr. Spencer could see his reaction. "What happened?"

"John didn't just walk by some random house. He was targeting the man inside."

"I need eyes there now," Curtis said, pulling into the street, weaving through the sparse traffic. "Is John still there?"

"Daniel and Renee are working on it now. And Curtis, they're blocking me out," she said, lowering her voice to just above a whisper.

"Blocking you out? Are you on lockdown?"

"No. I've got a workstation, but my permissions have been tightened up. I can see most of the older reports, but nothing new is coming in."

Curtis rubbed the back of his neck. "Alright. Just keep doing what you can. And if you get a chance, try and get some more information from the wonder twins."

"Okay, Lieutenant."

"Who is the target?" Curtis asked. "Who was John after?"

Miranda's keystrokes came through the speakers, like mild interference. "Monte Buchanan. He's retired, but Monte used to run an investment company. I can't get much more than that, though."

"Is he dead?" Curtis asked.

"I don't know," Miranda said. "All of the reports are outdated, and the—wait. I just got eyes on John."

"Where?" Curtis pulled into an empty lane and increased his speed.

"Last known position shows him a couple of miles from Buchanan's home, but that was almost an hour ago," Miranda said. *"And remember when I said you should hurry?"*

"Yeah."

"A team has been dispatched to pursue John. They're closing in on him fast."

***

The air clawed at John's throat. His chest ached and legs burned. Buchanan provided the name of the man at the top, and now his security detail was giving chase, barely a block away and closing fast. John pulled himself over a rusted gate, the freezing metal stinging his unprotected hands. The pistol in his jacket pocket dropped to the ground, clattering along the asphalt as his feet touched down.

The voices in the distance were converging on his position, but he took the precious few seconds to retrieve the weapon before continuing. The only thing that mattered now was escape, but his pursuers had changed somewhere in the night.

After leaving Monte Buchanan's house two of the man's security detail gave chase, but Monte was still alive, which would ensure that they would soon give up and return to their original protection detail. But then John made the mistake of slowing down, thinking he was safe enough to catch his breath. The men on his trail now were different. Private contractors fully kitted up and riding around in a pair of pickup trucks.

His considerable lead now down to only a few hundred feet, John forced his pursuers to close on foot, choosing a gated area of the industrial complex he reached, before the strength in his body waned. Faced with a fight against half a dozen well-trained and well-equipped mercenaries, John would need every trick in the book to even the odds.

The sky transitioned from the inky darkness to a lighter violet. The faintest orange band grew along the horizon. John had been on the run all night. Fighting the fatigue, he did his best to look at the only positive in the whole situation. If they wanted him dead or captured so badly, John knew that Monte had provided the exact name he had been searching for. Windham must have sent this goon squad, which meant he was the top of the food chain. He was the man that John needed to reach to end it all.

Numb hands gripped the VP40 pistol as John hunkered down behind the rusted husk of a delivery van. It had been scavenged for parts, but still afforded enough cover, while still allowing him to watch his pursuers close the distance. Less than a minute later, four men and two women stepped out of the shadows and into the pre-dawn glow.

Mercenaries. Each held a submachine gun and scanned the area over the weapon's sights. They spread out into a crescent formation, the outer soldiers moving ahead to funnel John into the middle, forcing him into the tiger's mouth. He needed to move to the outer edge of the group, but that would require a distraction. These mercs were real pros, advancing with coordination and discipline. John picked up an old pitted bolt, feeling the weight in his hand. He didn't want his diversion to be too loud. This was the type of crew that would catch on quickly.

John looked out to the other end of the industrial yard, and a stack of rotting pallets caught his eye. *Perfect.* Rolling the bolt between frozen fingertips, he leaned back and tossed it underhanded. The impact of rusty metal on old wood created the exact sound John had hoped for. It was soft, like someone accidentally bumping a weapon against something while trying to reposition.

All six guns drifted toward the sound in one smooth movement. John swung out to his left, staying in a combat crouch. He reached the outer edge of the mercenary pincer formation, only the deep shadows of the wall keeping him from view. The lead mercenary gave a signal, and the team advanced again, paying close attention to where John had thrown the bolt.

The man nearest to him approached, and John readied himself. Positioned just outside of their group, he hoped to wait for the merc to pass, so he could slip by and escape, but he would have to cover open ground where the woman furthest back would spot him. John's only option was to take out the wingman and work his way in, attempting to take out as many as he could before they spotted him.

CHAPTER
27

The Yukon rolled by Monte Buchanan's house, its engine emitting a low rumble, ready to ramp up at a moment's notice. Curtis noted the lack of police presence, but he saw two large unmarked SUVs parked at the gate, two men in suits standing guard. Not wanting to appear too interested or suspicious, he continued down the street, heading for John's last known location.

Glancing at his M4 carbine and plate carrier in the passenger seat, Curtis felt a strange sense of calm. It would be a tricky balancing act, trying to play peacekeeper to convince a fugitive to give himself up peacefully, while preventing an amped up crew from shooting first, like the overwatch team at the motel days earlier. Curtis flexed his hands gripping and releasing the steering wheel as he approached his destination.

He reached for his phone, ready to call Dr. Spencer when she called him first. He accepted the call and dropped the phone in the center console. "I was just about to call you, Doc. I'm getting close, and I just need to know—"

"It's a mercenary team," Miranda said, cutting him off.

She spoke in a hushed tone, and her breathing sounded labored.

"What do you mean?"

"The group dispatched to track John, it's not an official Hostile Response unit," she said.

Before he could ask how she knew, Miranda continued.

"I've been locked out of the official search, but all team allocations have to be logged, to ensure that no individual is tasked with multiple missions."

"And none of our guys have been tasked with the hunt," Curtis said.

"Exactly. I looked at the logs to see if the guys with you earlier were assigned to the mission," she said.

"So how do you know they're mercenaries?" Curtis asked.

"I, well I don't, but." She let her words trail off.

Curtis shared Miranda's same gut reaction, but there were far more profound ramifications than Miranda was probably thinking about.

"Where are you now?"

"I just stepped out of the lab. Daniel and Renee are still—"

"You can't go back in there," Curtis said. "We have no idea who knows what you just discovered. You can't trust anyone right now."

"What should I do? Where should I go?"

"First, go somewhere they wouldn't expect to find you. Not your quarters, they'll search there first if you're not in the lab."

"I should go see Director Van Pierce." Panic bled through Miranda's words now.

"No. Don't give them a way to track your movements," Curtis said. "Get out of the building if you can."

"Get out? What do you think is happening?"

"I don't know for sure, but none of this feels right."

"Are we in danger? Are they going to kill us?" Miranda asked.

"Doctor, you need to take a deep breath and relax," Curtis said. "I'm not sure what might be happening, but I've got a bad feeling about it. It may be nothing, but if you can hide, or escape, you should do that."

With his earlier team shooting at John unprovoked, and a group of hired guns giving chase now, Curtis had the confirmation he needed that it had to be a setup. This changed everything. Now he would be walking into a potential firestorm. The mercenaries would be looking to take John out, and if Curtis didn't intervene, he would be there to collect a body. He stole another glance at his loadout, a sense of unpreparedness now settling in.

With no information about the number of men after John or the weapons they were carrying, Curtis realized this was far more dangerous than he expected before heading out. He reached an intersection, looking both ways and trying to decide the best direction to take. Faint pops in the distance almost blended in with the Yukon's motor. He rolled the window down, a blast of cold air hitting his face. Curtis strained, leaning out the window when he heard another pair of pops followed by the unmistakable rattle of automatic gunfire. Without hesitation, he stepped on the gas and pulled the SUV toward the firefight.

"Doc, can you get out of sight?"

After a few moments of Miranda's rapid shallow breaths, she answered. *"I'm in the supply room. I don't think they'll look for me here."*

"Good. Keep your head down and don't come out unless someone that you absolutely trust comes for you," he said.

"Where are you going?" she asked.

"Into the storm."

***

Boots crunched on gravel and snow as his target closed. John saw the beam from the man's weapon light sweeping side to side, blasting away the darkness to uncover any threat. As he stepped past the junk pile hiding John, the light pivoted in his direction. John had to move fast, not wasting a moment to rethink his strategy.

He pushed forward, lit up by the beam's outer fringes, but avoiding the bright epicenter. His movement appeared more like a receding shadow, allowing John to chew up the distance before the mercenary could make sense of what was happening. In a smooth flowing sequence, John pinned the weapon to his opponent's body as he stepped behind him, wrapping his hand around, covering the entire lower half of the man's face.

With a sharp, wrenching yank, the mercenary's neck snapped, and his body collapsed. The muzzle of his CZ Scorpion clanged against a rusted barrel nearby, and two 800 lumen beams snapped over in John's direction. The mercenaries shouted and moved toward him. He pulled the pistol from his waistband and snapped a pair of shots at the closest. The .40 caliber rounds dropped the man, but he pulled himself behind cover before John could follow up.

John pivoted fast to engage the woman coming at him, but something obstructed his view of the VP40's front sight. *Stovepipe.*

The weapon failed to eject the last shot, and a piece of spent brass stuck out of the ejection port. He swiped a hand back, clearing the obstruction, and power stroked the slide to chamber the next round. Before he could line up his shot, the mercenary opened fire. John's bullet went high, and he fell back behind the piles of junk for cover.

The woman called to the rest of her team for support as she crouched, placing disciplined bursts around John's cover, keeping him pinned. He slid along his belly, moving far enough to avoid most of the suppressing fire. He had to engage now before the rest of the hired guns joined the fight.

Coming up on the far side of the junk pile he leveled his sights at the epicenter of the flashlight and brought his point of aim a bit higher. He pressed the trigger three times, the gun clicking on the final squeeze. The woman had stopped shooting, and her flashlight beam fell to the side, but there was enough light spilling over so John could see the double feed malfunction in his weapon.

He dropped back and tried to strip the magazine free to clear the chamber, but another attacker rounded the corner with a clear line of fire. John hurled the jammed pistol at his head. The steel slide struck the man's face, knocking a tooth out of the merc's mouth.

Staggering back on his heels, the man brought a hand up to his face and fired his Scorpion blind with the other. John was already sliding forward where the soldier with the broken neck still lay. He grabbed the dead man's SMG and fired a quick burst, still on his side. A mist of blood sprayed into the beam of the weapon's light as the merc fell. John rose to a kneeling position and pulled the gun to his shoulder. Or at least he attempted to. The CZ Scorpion resisted, its sling still wrapped around the dead mercenary's body.

John fired from the hip, emptying the mag, but the other two mercenaries swarmed him, spraying the area with long bursts, peppering his cover with 9-millimeter hollow points. He dropped the weapon and made a break for more cover, farther in the industrial graveyard. Bullets sparked all around him, and a round tore into the coat flapping behind him.

He half tripped, half dove behind another row of gutted vehicles, rolling the last meter as more rounds chewed up the ground behind him. Melting snow soaked one of his pant legs and a sleeve of his jacket. The cold seeped into his arms and legs, chilling him, even through the rush of adrenaline. Bullets rang off metal as the other woman issued orders to the soldier with her.

No weapons. Nowhere to hide. John looked around for something, anything that would help him turn the tables.

* * *

The Yukon's headlights illuminated two all black, unmarked pickup trucks. Curtis stomped the brake and fishtailed to a stop. He threw the door open and grabbed his rifle, pulling the plate carrier over his head and shoulders. The sounds of gunfire greeted him with muted pops in the distance.

Easing the charging handle back, he checked the chamber of his M4 and brought it up, making his way around his vehicle, keeping the weapon trained on the ghost trucks parked in front of the industrial facility. He reached the front gate and pressed himself up against the wall, stepping away to peer around.

Lieutenant Clarke adjusted the sling to move his rifle along his back as he jumped up to pull himself over the gate. His boots touched down, and he had the M4 back up and pointing forward. He moved toward the sounds of battle with hurried steps. Bullets struck metal, the pinging echoing and letting him know he was close to the fight.

Curtis sank lower, almost jogging with his knees bent as he stepped into the open yard, in front of the long-abandoned manufacturing plant. Flashlight beams waved around as combatants ran from cover to cover. Their muzzle flashes gave Curtis glimpses of wider areas. He dropped to one knee behind a concrete divider, propping his weapon up and sighting through his red dot sight, looking for John.

He found him further in the back where two mercenaries were firing on his position. The two split up and were making their way to a line of what used to be cars or trucks. Curtis shouldered his weapon and stepped out, moving to the next available cover. Movement out of the corner of his eye drew the M4's muzzle down and to the right.

One of the mercenaries had propped himself up against a metal drum. The injured man had his hand clutched to his chest, blood seeping from between shaky fingers. Curtis took a step toward him to help, but the man's face twisted into a scowl and he raised his weapon, a CZ Scorpion submachine gun. Lieutenant Clarke side-stepped and snapped his red dot up, just as the merc squeezed off a wild, one-handed burst. Curtis' M4 cracked twice, punching another pair of holes in the man's chest, one of the rounds going through his hand.

A woman's voice cut through the chaos, issuing orders to the other mercenary engaging John. Muzzle flashes lit up in the Lieutenant's direction, bullets hissing past and bouncing off the ground nearby. Curtis fired his weapon and ran forward, sliding along one knee, as he dropped behind the skeletal remains of a truck. He braced against the structure and continued firing at the man targeting him.

Curtis swapped magazines and surged ahead, throwing a wall of 5.56 NATO at his assailant, driving him back. John was pinned down, and every second Curtis delayed, was another chance for the hired guns to get the kill shot. He couldn't afford to let them drive the narrative after taking John out. He would have a hard enough time clearing the Ranger's name with him alive to tell his side of the story.

The mercenary let loose with another burst. Curtis felt the punch of a nine millimeter round making impact on his chest, but the ballistic plate had no trouble soaking up the kinetic energy. He pivoted and dropped behind a pile of scrap metal for a second before stepping back out re-engage the threat.

If I can't take this goon out fast, John is in grave danger.

No sooner did Curtis finish his thought that a furious roar joined chaotic chorus.

***

John's breath came out through gritted teeth. Death was rounding the corner, but he was prepared to make his attackers pay a hefty price for it. He shrugged his coat off and readied himself to rush the first merc to step into view. More shots came from further back, a much different sound than the Scorpions chattering and chipping away at his cover. It was a familiar report to John's ears. A pair of tight shots from an M4 carbine.

The woman stopped shooting only long enough to bark commands at the man with her, telling him to deal with the new shooter. John heard the merc's Scorpion crackle to life, and the M4 answered with authority. He raised his head up to see who joined the fight when the woman continued her assault. Sparks flashed out, and John retreated behind cover, just as he saw her approaching.

She circled around his position, only seconds away from clearing her line of fire. She stepped to the side, shooting quickly, relying too much on proximity and the weapon's rate of fire. Her rounds kicked up small gouts of pebbles, but John pivoted away a moment before. He took a bounding step toward a patch of tall yellowing grass. He hooked his thick fingers around the cold metal rim of a well-worn tire, half-hidden in the dead foliage.

John tensed his body, all of his muscles lengthening like a taut spring. He spun back toward the mercenary, his right arm trailing as he turned. Her muzzle tracked closer to him as he unleashed an angry shout that shook the air. John hurled the wheel like an enormous Olympic discus. The tire loomed huge in her vision and was on her before she could fire her weapon. The woman turned and shrugged a shoulder up, before the tire crashed into her body, knocking the wind from her and sending her sprawling to the ground.

John lunged in, but the mercenary was too fast. She rolled back over a shoulder, coming to a low crouch. Steel flashed, as the woman pulled a karambit, the wicked talon-shaped blade slicing through the air. She scrambled to her feet, whipping the knife in small figure-eight motions, keeping John back. The point bit into the flesh on his forearm, and he backed away. She timed a back step flawlessly, and put more than enough room between them, bringing her firearm back into the fight.

John wrenched the door of the nearest vehicle open and ducked behind it. The mercenary's SMG ripped into the barrier with a heavy staccato rhythm, the door unable to stop many of the rounds from punching through, then the firing ceased. A spent magazine clattered to the ground. John ripped the door from its rusted hinges and rushed his attacker again. She was already slapping a full magazine into the weapon when she looked up at him.

John's feet slipped on the loose gravel, making it difficult to find purchase. His makeshift door shield wouldn't do much to stop the incoming fire, but his legs continued to push, as he bore down on the woman. The merc sent the bolt home and shouldered the Scorpion.

Thunder clapped from his left, a strangely distant sound. The woman's body lurched, and her head snapped violently to the side. A mist sprayed out, catching the golden rays of the rising sun. John watched the merc's body topple over in slow motion. He snapped his gaze in the direction of the shooter.

Lieutenant Curtis Clarke approached with smooth steps, maintaining his point of aim, keeping the M4 braced up against his shoulder.

"It's over, John. We're going back to the base to clear this whole situation up."

CHAPTER
28

Curtis closed the gap, keeping his weapon trained on John. "Keep your hands where I can see them."

"You're making a mistake, Lieutenant. Someone is framing me." John raised his arms, keeping his hands at shoulder height.

"We can discuss this back at HRD."

"Who do you think is behind this? Your thugs tried to kill me earlier, what makes you think they weren't the ones that sent this hit squad after me?"

"I'll be there to make sure you get a fair shake," Curtis said, keeping his M4 up. He retrieved a pair of plastic flex cuffs from his duty belt.

"Did Van Pierce send you? Just call him, and let me talk to him," John said.

"The Director has been relieved of command and restricted to quarters." Curtis motioned in a small circle with the cuffs. "Turn around and lace your fingers behind your head."

John complied, his feet scraping the loose pebbles as he turned. "What is your gut telling you, Clarke. Why would they want Van Pierce out of the picture? You and I both know, as the director, he had the pull to end this whole thing."

"We'll clear this all up," Curtis said. "We'll get you back, explain the whole situation, and once Van Pierce is back in control, everyone responsible will face the repercussions of their actions."

"I suppose that means me too, right?" John asked, with a dry chuckle, shoulders sagging with fatigue.

Curtis grabbed his wrist, pulling to loop one end of the cuffs on and John spun to face him. With a stiff palm strike to the side of the M4, he knocked it free from Curtis' grasp. Wasting no time, John grabbed the ends of the ballistic plate in Curtis' chest rig and tossed him to the side.

Before Curtis could roll to his feet, John was on him, slinging a hammering right hand to the ribs, between the front and back armor plates. Curtis ducked the follow-up hook and answered with a stiff right cross and front kick to push the mountain of a man back.

"I don't want to fight you, John."

"Not your call, kid," John said, already bridging the gap.

They fought hard, Curtis landing two blows for every one of John's, but the Army Ranger's considerable size and strength advantage soon came into play. John hurled Curtis bodily through the air, and the smaller man impacted against a pile of crates. Curtis barely ducked under a blow that would have ended the fight, before wrapping his arms around John's waist, driving forward and pushing the big man back on his heels.

John twisted and shoved him off, but this time as Curtis came up to a crouch, he drew his M9 pistol and held it steady. "Stop, John. Look me in the eye if you don't think I'll shoot you."

Shoulders hunched, breath puffing out in visible clouds, John ran his tongue across the corner of his mouth, tasting blood. He fixed his gaze into Curtis' eyes and straightened his posture, holding his hands up near his chest, palms out.

"Lieutenant, I have reason to believe there is a level of corruption above the Hostile Response Division," he said, appealing to Curtis' professional nature. "Someone in the government is exerting his or her influence to frame me, and shut Marvin Van Pierce's group down."

Curtis rose to his feet, his aim never wavering from John's chest. He returned the burning stare, the internal struggle more evident now than ever.

"I have a name," John said. "Pryce Windham. He's the one at the top. He must have some influence in the government."

John pulled his shoulders back a little more and let his hands drift down slowly. "Curtis. I need to follow through with this. We can't trust the HRD right now."

The seconds stretched out, pulling out to minutes, hours in John's mind. He had an opening to move in and disarm the operative, but he needed Curtis to see his truth, so he could pursue Windham without the Lieutenant on his trail.

Curtis shook his head, breathed out a long exhale, and lowered his weapon. "I can't clear your name like this, Stone. I can't even keep them from coming after you."

"I'm not asking you to run interference. I just need you to stand down and let me go."

Curtis de-cocked his Beretta and held it out to John. "My SUV is out front. The key is still in the ignition."

John paused for a moment before reaching out to grab the weapon. "Thank you, Lieutenant Clarke."

"Believe me, it's the very least I can do."

"That's all I ask," John said, tucking the pistol into his waistband.

Sirens wailed in the distance, and a low steady thumping joined in. "You better get out of here, John."

He nodded at Curtis before heading toward the entrance.

The GMC Yukon's engine growled to life before fading into the distance, replaced by the pulsing vibration of a helicopter hovering overhead. Over the screaming sirens of the approaching authorities, Curtis felt the hum of his phone. He pulled it out and looked down at the screen, showing the name of the caller.

"You sly dog," Curtis said, smirking as he accepted the call.

***

Pryce leaned his elbow on his desk, squeezing his temples with his thumb and forefinger. "Send him in," he said, clicking the intercom off. He knew what information the man in charge of managing *assets* in the field was about to tell him. Pryce had already received the news from Mr. Gordon only moments earlier.

The office door swung open, and the portly man stepped in, stopping short as Pryce's enforcer blocked the path on his way out. The man bobbled his head several times, a weak apologetic gesture, as he shuffled to the side to let Mr. Gordon out of the room.

"Mr. Windham," he said, another series of bobs following.

Straightening in his chair, Pryce placed his hands on the desk, one over the other. "What is it?"

"The, uh, I mean, Baker and Reed called. John Stone has escaped. Again"

Pryce closed his eyes for several seconds and blew a breath out through his nose. "Where is he now?"

The man tugged at his collar in a cartoonish gesture and swallowed before responding. "We don't know. He appears to have had some help from one of his previous Hostile Response Division colleagues. A Lieutenant Curtis Clarke."

He didn't want this sad song and dance to continue, fast losing patience with the incompetent man. Pryce waved him away, no longer interested in talking. He sat back in the chair, resting his steepled fingers on his lips, forcing himself to take slow deep breaths to calm down.

John Stone was a thorn in his side. It should have been a simple matter to remove him from the equation and keep him out of play, while he dismantled the HRD. Marvin Van Pierce was already out of the way, yet his influence continued to haunt

Pryce. He looked down at his right hand, balled up so tight the flesh along the edges of his palm were a bright red, his nails digging into the tissue.

Relaxing, he rubbed his hands together and stood, just as Mr. Gordon came back into the office.

"Perfect, just the man I wanted to see," Pryce said. "Find out everything Buchanan said to Stone. I want to know if that fat little ferret told him too much. And mobilize one of our remote assets. Have them start a search for John Stone."

Gordon nodded. "And Buchanan?"

Pryce chewed on his lower lip for a moment and let out a small sigh. "Unharmed, for now. We'll need him still, after all of this is over." He placed his hands in his pockets. "But make sure you remind him of his grievous error if he did, in fact, say more than he should have."

* * *

"Ankles crossed! Lace your fingers behind your head!"

Curtis complied with the commands shouted over the *whumping* of the overhead chopper. The sun was up now, but its warmth did little to comfort the Lieutenant. The chill that ran up his spine had nothing to do with the weather. He saw the look in

John's eyes when he had him in his sights. Curtis knew deep down what John said had to be true, but something inside wouldn't let him fully believe it.

But after a face to face encounter with the man, he saw only truth. It was John's truth, but Curtis could see that John believed it with every fiber of his being. His sole focus was to bring John in, alive. He told himself it was to get to the bottom of the whole situation. That it was about letting John tell his side of the story, in the hopes that it would help during a trial. But Curtis knew that he was a fool for thinking that way, with all the evidence stacking up the way it did. John's eyes said more than his words and helped Curtis see what he refused to believe.

Someone wedged a boot between Curtis' crossed feet and pinned his hands to his head. Another soldier checked him for weapons, tossing the knife in his belt away and pulling the spare magazines from his pouches. Another man circled around, keeping the M4's muzzle at a low ready. He probed the crushed remains of Curtis' mobile phone.

"We've got Clarke in custody now," he said, as one of the others secured Curtis' hands behind his back with flex cuffs. "He made a call before we got to him, but the phone is smashed."

Hands hooked under his arms, hoisting Curtis to his feet.

"Bring me the SIM card. We can get everything we need from that."

Curtis tensed when he heard Daniel's voice over the radio. He was right to tell Miranda to hide when he did. After locking her out, he knew Renee and Daniel were following the orders of the people John hoped to uncover, but hearing his voice just now let Curtis know he couldn't be trusted anymore. Curtis berated himself for not approaching the situation differently.

Alone and outgunned, with a small army tracking him down, John had no one to help him find Pryce Windham.

CHAPTER
29

Parker stood up in his cell, leaning his head against the bars to see who they were bringing in now. "John?"

"Step back, Lewis," the MP said, escorting someone into the cell next to Parker.

The door clicked shut, and Curtis stuck his hands through the slot in the door so the guard could remove the flex cuffs binding his wrist. "Hey, kid. You find a way to hack these bars open?" he said with a wry smile.

"Lieutenant Clarke?" Parker pressed himself up against the bars again. "Did you find John?"

Curtis paused before answering. "Yes. And no. It's complicated, and I'm not so sure we should be discussing it here."

"I suppose you're right," Parker said. "Is he okay?"

Parker heard the man chuckle.

"We're talking about the same man that had a building dropped on him barely a month ago," Curtis said.

"He's tougher than he looks," Parker said with nervous laughter.

Cutis let out a bellowing laugh. "He looks like an Abrams tank with a beard. I can't imagine how much tougher he can get."

"It's good that his mustache has a buddy."

"It's probably the only thing keeping him warm."

Parker sat on the concrete. "Do you know where he's going now?"

"I think it's better for him that I don't," Curtis said.

The door at the end of the hall opened and closed again. Parker tried to see the person approaching, with the same futile method of mashing his face against steel.

"What are you doing here, Doctor Spencer," Curtis said. "I told you to get out if you could."

"I know, but when I saw them bringing you in." Miranda let her words hang.

"Miranda, were you able to find John with the mob recognition mods?" Parker asked.

Dr. Spencer stepped away from Curtis' cell so she could see Parker. "No. Well, I mean yes we did, originally," she said.

"That was when I found him the first time," Curtis said.

"He must have figured out what we were doing, and changed his behavior to avoid the algorithms," Miranda said.

"Huh, I never even thought of that," Parker said. "So what are your plans to find him now?"

She stepped closer to his cell. "I'm locked out."

"She shouldn't even be here," Curtis said. "Daniel and Renee are helping whoever is trying to shut us down."

"Is Doctor Spencer in danger?" Parker asked, real concern in his voice.

"I don't know," she said. "They haven't been looking for me, but I no longer have access to the system."

"That's why you need to lay low until you can get out," Curtis said. "We don't know who's involved, or how."

"He's right," Parker said. "It's not worth the risk. We don't even know who John is looking for."

"Pryce Windham," Curtis said.

"Who is that?" Miranda asked.

"That's the name John gave me. It's the man he's looking for."

* * *

The temperature in the computer lab almost matched the dreary winter day outside. Dr. Spencer poked her head in quickly, checking to make sure the room was empty before slipping through the door and padding to the far corner. She scooped an older laptop on the desk, tucking it under one arm before heading back out.

It wasn't connected to the processor web running the mob recognition program because it lacked the raw horsepower they needed to churn through the data. It would be perfect for what she needed. Unmonitored, underestimated, and practically invisible to the system. Miranda straightened her posture and strode down the hall, like she had no worries, or wasn't doing anything questionable.

Curtis was right, however. She needed to find somewhere to avoid attention and lay low. But sitting in a hiding spot, hoping to elude everyone walking by wasn't how she intended to spend her time. Miranda made it back to the supply room and side-stepped by the stacks of boxes, into the little hollow she prepared.

The fan whined, filling the small room with the plastic sound. She didn't know what to look for exactly, but she had a name, and that was enough information to start digging. Pryce Windham didn't appear much in the outside world's news stories or official filings, but the HRD network oddly had a database on the man and his influence in the corporate world.

His name appeared many times, connected to over a dozen smaller companies. Nothing stood out as unusual, but many of those smaller entities frequently did business with companies flagged by the HRD. Money laundering, or moving assets from one name to another, to cover transactions.

She leaned to the side, looking at the door to make sure no one had come in. She would be able to hear anyone opening the door, but her clandestine actions mere making her paranoid. Miranda pulled up a secure connection to a remote drive and dumped a few essential files. Nothing that would take too long to transfer, but enough to look into later. Pulling out her phone and thumbing through the contacts, she selected a name typed up a quick text message, letting him know what to look for, and what she had learned from Curtis. The confirmation *whoosh* sound felt almost soothing, letting her know that her message in a bottle made it out safely.

Miranda pressed her hands together and held them in front of her mouth, tucking her thumbs under her chin. "Let's keep digging," she said, sliding the laptop closer again.

Fingers danced across the keys, bouncing and sliding along the touchpad as she continued her deep dive into the mystery man. She had more files queued up, ready to push to her remote drive when someone pounded on the door.

"Who's in there?" A gruff voice asked.

"I just told you, it's Doctor Spencer," Renee said, barely audible from the hallway.

"Doctor Spencer, I need you to step out now. Please don't make me kick the door down."

Miranda chewed on her thumbnail for a few seconds, a million possibilities whipping through her mind, all a useless blur of thoughts. "Okay. I'll come out." She closed all of the connections and lowered the laptop's display, tucking it further back. "Please don't shoot me." She closed her eyes, wincing at the ridiculous statement.

She turned the handle pulled it open slowly, seeing a man in uniform, towering over her. He placed a gentle hand on the back of her elbow and eased her out of the room. Renee stepped around her and stepped into the supply room, emerging seconds later with the laptop.

"Checking your Facebook page?" she asked with a smug look of self-satisfaction. "You think you're so slick, Doctor, but Daniel and I knew you couldn't be trusted. You thought you could sneak all that data out of here?"

Miranda's eyes widened.

"That's right, We locked down your connection. Did you think you could push almost a terabyte of data without us seeing it?"

Dr. Spencer only now realized that Renee was talking about the files she had queued up for the second push. The first few files had already made it out. She narrowed her mouth and looked down at the floor, trying to hide any sign that she may have succeeded.

"Lock her up with the others," Renee said, walking back to the computer labs.

***

Adrenaline long faded, the pain and stiffness settled deep into John's body. The sun did little to warm him during the few times the clouds didn't actually darken the sky. He drove Curtis' SUV as long as he felt he could, before choosing to ditch the vehicle. The Yukon would be compromised, anyway. Too big, too easy to spot. The only bright spot was the rugged tablet stashed in the back pouch, behind the driver's seat. John didn't know when he would be able to get access to a computer to search for more information about Pryce, and he knew using the HRD device was a risk, but finding the man responsible for framing him was more important right now.

At least he thought it would be a benefit. What John discovered was the man he was researching kept much of his activities out of the public eye. He was a phantom, unseen or unheard of in the real world. The only mentions were the few times when Pryce exercised his stock options from one of the many companies he maintained.

John's fingers tightened, and plastic creaked against glass, threatening to crack. The frustration welled up. He leaned back against the brick wall in the back parking lot, behind a strip mall. The cold was all-encompassing and only added to the hopelessness that threatened to pull him under. He closed his eyes and looked up when the tablet chirped and buzzed.

His heart raced, he worried that he pushed his luck. The device was still logged in with Curtis' credentials, giving John access to the regular outside network, as well as anything in the HRD network. He avoided looking at the files on the internal servers, to avoid raising any red flags. But it appeared that they may have noticed, which meant they could track him through the device.

He reached for the power switch, but the alert message caught his eye. It was a message sent to Curtis, but the excerpt displayed on the small popup tab said *Hey, John. How's the weather?*

John stood up, his eyes darting back and forth. Did they already find him? Were they descending on his position now? The desire to check what had been sent outweighed the urge to trash the tablet and run. John opened the app and selected the message, checking to see who it was from.

"Why would I expect anything less," he said chuckling with relief.

The message from Marvin Van Pierce was brief, with only a short greeting and several addresses listed. John looked at the locations looking for some type of hint, or clue about the relevance of the different places. He input the destinations in the mapping app on the tablet, trying to decipher a pattern when he finally understood what the message meant.

Each of the addresses was roughly the same distance apart from the industrial facility where Curtis gave him the keys to the Yukon. The addresses gave John two possibilities. The first was that it appeared that the people running the HRD now had no reliable method to track him. The second was that MVP wanted John to visit one of the locations, but wasn't sure which direction he may have headed after leaving the firefight.

The closest destination was a few hours away on foot. If he left now, he would be able to reach it before sundown, giving him enough light, and warmth, to keep an eye on the location to see if it was a potential trap. He didn't expect to see the director at any of the sites, unless he already knew which point John would head for, only sending the rest as a smoke screen.

Even though that's the type of clever ruse Van Pierce was capable of, John still felt that was a long-shot. He spent another couple of minutes looking at the map, memorizing the other locations, just in case he needed to hit all of them. His thumb slid up to the power button, holding it down for several seconds to shut the device down. John thought about smashing the tablet to prevent anyone from finding him, but he considered hanging on to it.

The reflection in the black screen was worn and weather-beaten. John's beard had grown in thick and full in the month since he had finally seen his mission of vengeance through by taking out Warren Ratcliffe. John brushed the bushy beard with dried and cracked hands. There was still one more target to hit. One more man to bring down.

With a firm grasp on either end of the tablet, John flexed his hands and wrists, snapping it in half, sending a spray of glass and plastic outward. He stacked the two halves together and dropped them into a dumpster.

This could very well be a trap. But given the limited amount of information about Pryce Windham, John had already decided to take the bait. The Beretta M9 pressed into his midsection as he adjusted his pants, pulling his t-shirt over the grip, hiding the pistol from casual onlookers.

CHAPTER
30

The Air stairs bounced gently as Pryce stepped off the plane. He smiled and waved at the waiting car, fastening the bottom button of his jacket. Pulling the collar closer to stave off the icy wind, he crossed the distance to the waiting vehicle, as the driver stepped out. Pryce's smile faded when the man he had expected to open the rear door, approached him instead, with a phone in his hand.

"What's the meaning of this?" he asked, speaking at the car and ignoring the man in front of him.

The driver's dark lenses hid his gaze, as he handed Pryce the phone. "The call is for you, sir."

With a scowl, he snatched the phone and held it to his ear.

"I'm very sorry, Mr. Windham, but I felt the need to come here and tell you in person that—"

"One could hardly consider a phone call *in person*. Let's just discuss what this is really about," he said.

"I truly apologize for the embarrassment, but my associates and I just can't risk being seen with you at the moment," the woman on the call said. *"Your name has been coming up a lot in queries directed at our organizations lately."*

"When?" he asked, truly perplexed.

"Three or four times in the past eight hours, which is concerning enough. But within the last hour over a dozen requests have come in through our servers. Even you must agree that is a bit excessive."

"Who is it? Who is looking for me?"

"Mr. Windham, I do apologize for this inconvenience," she said.

"Listen to me, you little lap dog. If you think I'm just going to—"

"Don't presume to treat me like one of your secretaries, Pryce. I was already on my way to pick you up when this all happened." Her tone changed dramatically. *"I've got a message from Ms. Flair and the others. Clean your mess up. Deal with this John Stone. And until you do, you are not to contact us in any way."*

His face flushed, his teeth gritted. Pryce tried to fire back a response when the line clicked, ending the call. His fingers tightened on the phone, digging into the flesh around his fingers. The driver stood tall, holding a hand out for the phone.

The audacity of this hired muscle. A wage slave thinking he was better than Pryce. The self-satisfied look on the driver's face made him furious. He stepped to one side and threw the phone at the car. It struck the armored door panel and bounced to the tarmac, cracking on impact. Pryce turned and walked back to the plane, twirling his finger in the air in a gesture to let the crew know they were leaving.

Pryce's assistant jogged over as he reached the plane. "Sir, where are we going?"

"Get us off the ground now. I'll tell you where we're going once I figure it out."

"We're not cleared for takeoff. We can't just get back into the air without a destination, or itinerary or something," the assistant said.

Pryce grabbed the slighter man's collar and pulled him close. "We're going to Wyoming. Get me in the air now."

The man nodded and hurried into the plane.

Pryce climbed the stairs and walked back to his seat, as the pilot's arguing bled out from the cockpit. He settled into the leather chair and dialed his phone, calling his head of security.

"Call it off. Stop the search and bring everyone back to the estate. If John Stone wants me, he'll have to get through an army to do it."

***

John rubbed one forearm and then the other, trying to brush away the cold. His breath puffed out in visible clouds as the sun dipped below the horizon, the temperature following it. The destination he chose was a multi-level parking lot, two floors from the top, tucked away in a back corner. He climbed in through the side, slipping under the taut steel cable meant to keep cars in, not people out.

For the past hour, he crouched in the shadows far away from the stairs or elevators, avoiding as many people as possible. The only vehicle he saw was an older model silver sedan parked in the spot indicated on MVP's message. He watched the car, but no one had been on this floor the entire time. John made a note of the cameras mounted around. If anyone was watching this place, they could be monitoring from a remote location, ready to spring the trap.

His hand instinctively found the butt of his pistol, but he had to make the conscious effort to relax, keeping his hands in view. Rolling his shoulders forward, he gave himself a slight hunch and walked with shorter shuffling steps than usual. If the mob recognition software was running, he didn't want to make their job any easier.

At the passenger side of the car, John glanced in, seeing no one inside. There was an index card on the driver seat, but nothing else of note. He circled around, keeping a slow, casual pace and without a pause, pulled the front door open, picking up the card and settling into the seat.

John looked at the blank side of the card for a second before flipping it over. There was a key taped to it, and a single word scrawled in marker. *Trunk*. He stepped out, walked to the back, and looked around the parking structure, to make sure no passersby happened to be strolling through. Turning the key between his numb fingers, John unlocked the trunk and eased the lid open, leaning to one side to look through the gap.

Once opened all the way, he looked down at the duffle bag tucked along one side. John pulled the zipper open and dug around inside. Sitting on top of everything else, he saw a thick jacket, a pair of gloves, and a set of extra clothes. Before continuing, John pulled the coat out, slid his arms through and zipped the front up. The warmth he felt was an immediate boost to his morale. He pocketed the gloves for later and continued digging.

It didn't take long for John to realize this was definitely a care package, sent by Van Pierce after he must have spoken with Lieutenant Clarke. He pulled out a Kydex holster for the Beretta he had taken from Curtis. John slipped the gun inside and secured it to his waist.

Van Pierce also left a hundred dollars in cash, some bottled water, a monocular, and a pre-paid flip phone with a single contact already saved in the list. John didn't recognize the number but had no doubt it, too, was a burner phone. He zipped the bag up, pulled it out, and closed the trunk. Tossing it into the passenger seat, John pulled the seatbelt across his body. The car coughed and rumbled to life, and he cranked the heater to the highest setting, before pulling the phone out again.

After three rings Van Pierce picked up. *"John?"*

"It's me. Curtis said you were being detained. How did you get out?"

"I wasn't exactly detained. Just confined to quarters and relieved of command," he said. *"I was able to convince the young man keeping tabs on me that the whole overwatch thing was wrong. Lucky for me, he sort of saw things my way, before he looked the other way while I slipped out."*

"I have to say, it's nice to hear your voice, Director, but the care package you left for me is much nicer."

"Man, I knew you were tough, but I didn't think you were also crafty enough to get as far as you have with the number of resources they've been devoting to track you down."

"All things considered, I would rather not be in this position," John said. "I really need to know what is going on."

"Well, you're in luck, John," Van Pierce said. *"I had to make an educated guess about which location you would choose, so I'm not too far from your current location."*

"I'm guessing you know where I am based on the number I'm calling from. But how do you know I'm not already on the move?"

"Like I said, crafty."

CHAPTER
31

John pressed both hands against the wall and leaned under the shower, letting the heat loosen his muscles and ease the tension throughout his body. Van Pierce left him enough cash in the care package to get a motel room, and John seized the opportunity for the first shower and hot meal in days. He toweled off and got dressed in the still warm bathroom, putting on the extra clothes from the duffel bag.

Dressed and refreshed, he tucked the holstered pistol into his waistband and pulled the jacket on. The bag was light, nearly empty now, swinging from his shoulder as he left the room. His journey to rendezvous with MVP was short and uneventful, but that didn't stop him from continually watching, his head on a swivel.

John half expected the meeting to occur at a park, where Van Pierce would be sitting on a bench, feeding ducks. Or in the far corner of a diner, *hiding in plain sight*. But given the situation, they both felt it best to avoid any and all surveillance. Stashing the car in a nearby parking lot, he dumped the bag with his old clothes inside.

Marvin Van Pierce's car sat on the far end, under a broken light, in a pool of darkness. John jogged up but kept his hand near the pistol as he approached. Unable to see through the heavily tinted windows, he circled around to the front, still hesitant but approaching nonetheless. He trusted MVP at this point but letting his guard down now would be foolish.

John drew his weapon and kept it hidden behind his leg. He opened the door with his left hand and slid inside, sitting down with the Beretta resting on his lap as he closed the door. Though not as cold as the outside temperature, John expected the interior to be much warmer.

"You like it chilly, don't you?"

MVP smiled and shrugged. "Running the engine while I waited just felt like a waste of gas. Who knows if we'll need every last drop."

"Thank you for the care package, by the way," John said. "I was about to call it quits if I had to go another day without a decent pair of gloves."

"Yeah, I figured those bear paws of yours were pretty sensitive. But that was just the appetizer. You're here for the main course."

John tucked the pistol back into the holster. "Alright, you've got my attention."

Van Pierce's smile grew. "Well, let's just say that Lieutenant Clarke may have mentioned a name to a certain doctor we know, and before the new HRD overlords locked her up, she passed some useful information about this person of interest."

"Pryce Windham."

"This is going to make your day, Stone," Marvin said. "Your little escapade has helped shine a light on that cockroach, and all the other pests he runs with. You've got him scared."

"Scared isn't enough," John said. "I need him taken down for good. Either a bullet or a gavel, he needs to fall."

"We can't build a case by ourselves. Especially not since we're both wanted men now."

John's face hardened. "Then we need to get our hands on him, and find out everything he knows."

"You're spoiling the surprise. I just got a message from a friend in the FAA. I know where Windham is headed."

***

"Drop me off here," Marvin said.

John pulled the car over, stopping in front of an abandoned fire station. Weeds had overtaken the front facade of the structure, yellowed by the cold, but still tall and thick.

"What is this place?" he asked.

"This is my stop. Take this key and use my room to get a full night's sleep," Van Pierce said. "It's a long drive to Windham's mountain estate, and you're going to need all the strength you can get."

"What are you going to do?"

"Just some light shopping," Marvin said. "Scout the area and I'll meet you later. But don't do anything crazy. At least not until I get there."

John watched the HRD director jog up the path and disappear inside the old building. Marvin left a file folder on the seat. The pages inside were the printouts he provided, giving John all the information he needed about Pryce's home. He looked down at the key card, tucked inside the small paper sleeve with the motel's address written on the back. They had been driving for hours, and the opportunity for a few hours of sleep sounded far too good to pass up.

CHAPTER
32

John was awake and on the road, the sun barely up and beaming in through the driver side window. Even in his broken and worn out state, he was only able to sleep for six hours. His body felt stiff and sore, but the rest filled him with a renewed vigor, driven by the mission to reach Pryce Windham. To stand face to face with the man and bring him to justice, or take him down.

It took the better part of the morning to reach Wyoming, and another couple of hours to make it to the outskirts of Windham's property. Thick snow blanketed everything, coating the trees with fresh powder overnight. But today John hardly felt the cold. A fire inside kept him warm. Part anger, part anticipation.

"Get a hold of yourself, John. This isn't over yet." His hands tightened on the wheel as he pulled the car over.

He killed the engine and sat still for a moment before reaching over for the files Marvin left for him. Several of the pages were printouts of satellite photos, showing the layout of the land. John focused on two of the pages showing the path up to the primary structure. The distance from the road to Windham's estate looked to be over a kilometer.

Trekking through knee-deep snow over rough terrain made the approach difficult. Tracing the best path along the broad clearing with his finger, John noticed a small structure tucked into the tree line. He brought the page closer, unsure of what he was looking at. It was a small flat area above the snow, likely a wooden platform.

He sat back in his seat, stretching his arms out in front, trying to see the *big picture*. It was the perfect spot, affording a clear, unobstructed view, right at a choke point where towering walls of rock closed in. *That's where I'd put a sniper,* he thought. *Of course, it would work better with overlapping fields of view.*

Running his finger to the other side of the walls, he spotted a corner poking out from under a tree. "Bingo." A second platform had been constructed on the other side of the clearing, perfect for use as watchtowers. With a sniper on each, they would be able to dissuade any aggressive approach on foot. The roads leading up to Pryce's home were more than likely under heavy patrol, making the long trek up the back of the mountain the best method of getting in.

The photos showed the platforms empty, likely taken hours or even days before Pryce had returned to hole up. It was worth the risk to traverse through the trees to get at least a small glimpse of the closest platform. Waltzing up the side of a mountain right into the line of fire would be bad for the mission at hand.

John instinctively pulled his sleeve back to check his watch, seeing only a bare wrist. Not having a watch felt strange. Relying on a burner phone to check the time even more so. Van Pierce never gave him a definite time, but the last text message said he was on the way. That was over an hour ago.

"Might as well get something done while I'm here."

Pocketing the monocular, John circled away from the road leading to the clearing, heading deep into the trees. The light gray jacket and pants MVP provided proved somewhat useful in the snow. Not quite a camouflage pattern, it still helped to smooth his silhouette with all the snow around.

Relying heavily on the magnification of the small handheld scope, John covered only a couple hundred meters to edge closer to the clearing. Belly crawling through the deep snow would help keep him hidden, but he would have to be careful about making a man-sized trench that one of the spotters could see after he left.

Even with the optic's 10x magnification, John could only see the faintest outline of the nearest platform. Undoubtedly if they had anyone posted as a lookout, they would have far more powerful eyes. He couldn't get any closer without risking being spotted. Several more agonizing minutes passed before he could see something moving. A sliver of shadow wavered in his sight. Someone was standing on the structure, looking down.

John struggled to sharpen the image in his mind when he caught the glint off of a scope. It had come from far too low to be in the standing man's hands. A sniper was lying prone, scanning the area, and John could feel the shooter's eye fixed on him. He lowered his head closer to the snow and pulled the monocular under his body, slowing his breathing and waiting for the inevitable impact.

After two full deep breaths, it was clear that the sniper wasn't preparing to shoot. Still, John would have to be careful about how he backed away. He still needed to make some attempt to cover his tracks, but in a way that didn't require any sudden movements. With slow, methodical backsliding, and long swipes of his arms, he pulled back enough to get to his feet and head down to wait for Van Pierce.

* * *

"For a second there, I thought I was about to miss out on all the fun," Marvin said, leaning against the fender of a matte white and gray H1 Hummer.

John brushed the snow from his pants and jacket. "Looks like you brought the party favors, so I had to wait."

"So what are we looking at up there?" Marvin asked. "Welcoming committee?"

"Couple of doormen," John said. He walked over to the car and reached into the opened window to retrieve the overhead photo printouts. "These two positions here are elevated platforms. There's a sniper on this one, and I can only assume that there is another trigger on the other side as well."

"Wow, I guess we shouldn't be surprised that Windham is a bit skittish about uninvited guests."

"Speaking of surprises, what's all this about?" John asked jutting a whiskered chin toward the Hummer.

"Oh, that? Like I said, shopping. Just needed to pick up a few supplies for the job," Van Pierce said. He walked around to the back and opened the tailgate, pulling out an M16A2, with a grenade launcher mounted under the barrel.

"Now that I can get behind."

"This little beauty is mine. Your gear is back there," Marvin pointed to the rest of the equipment in the back.

John's eyes widened at the large crates filling most of the cargo area. "Where did you get that?"

"I know a guy that knows a guy," Marvin said. "So what's the plan, then? How are we going to deal with the snipers?"

"Well, even with all this," John gestured into the truck, "they would spot us coming from a mile away. Literally. I'm guessing Pryce would drop a small army on our heads if that were the case."

"Stealth, then?"

"If I can get up to the closest platform, and take out the shooter and spotter, we would have a pretty clear path along the south edge of the property," John said. "The snipers have an overlapping field of fire, but once we're at the platform, they would have to be looking directly at the other team to see us, and I doubt they're swinging the scopes out that far."

"Need some company?" Marvin inserted a magazine into his rifle and worked the charging handle.

"I think I can manage. Just wait down here for me to come back," John said.

"Sounds good," Marvin said. "I'll need your help to lug all of this gear once we start the main event."

CHAPTER
33

Clearing one side, so he and Van Pierce could reach Pryce Windham's *estate* unnoticed, posed the least amount of risk, John reasoned. The heavily wooded area thinned, as the rock wall to his left rose and angled in, forcing him closer and closer to the tree line. He was crouched, moving with careful steps to avoid anything that would give away his position.

Pressing his back against the rock wall, John pulled out the monocular. Blurred swaths of trees painted over the view, but he could see enough of the platform from there. His hand rested on the butt of the Colt 1911 in a drop leg holster. It was one of the toys MVP brought along, swapping it out for the Beretta, along with the KA-BAR knife strapped to his chest.

There was no doubt that it wouldn't be too difficult to get close enough to reach out and touch them with the big .45 caliber rounds, but John needed to clear the path quietly, which meant the blade would be doing the brunt of his work. He unsnapped the KA-BAR and clutched it in his hand, belly crawling the rest of the way to the base of the platform.

A set of wooden steps came down from the perch, pressed along the back edge. John eased up the stairs, settling his foot on each wooden plank before shifting his weight forward at an excruciatingly slow pace. His head reached the base of the platform, and he fixed his gaze on the two men watching the path below, unaware that death was stalking them.

John took the same measured approach, settling each foot down, establishing a firm grip on his knife as he closed the gap. He reached out with his left, holding the knife close to his body with his right, ready to clamp a hand around the spotter's mouth and pull him into the blade. He stepped closer, and a faint metallic *thunk* sounded under his boot. It was like a thunderclap in John's ears.

The spotter spun, his free hand falling to the grip of the HK UMP45 strapped to his shoulder. John pounced, driving the tip of his blade forward. The spotter brought his left hand into the path, more instinct than skill, and the knife punctured flesh, plastic, and glass. The man's hand and spotter's scope stopped the KA-BAR.

With the blade stuck, John hammered the man with a huge left cross, whipping the spotter's head to the side. He turned and hurled the man to the edge of the platform, and wheeled around. Just in time to see the sniper already up in a combat crouch, unholstering the pistol on his hip.

John ate up the gap with one long stride and swatted the weapon away with a massive hand, sending it flying into the snow. The sniper drove his shoulder forward and attempted to hoist John off of his feet. The mountainous man sank his two hundred forty pound frame. The soldier may have well been trying to lift two hundred forty tons. John dug into the sniper's ribs with thundering right hooks, each turning the man to the side, and eliciting a grunt, as man's strength faded.

The mercenary stepped away and threw a punch, landing flush across John's jaw. The man's eyes, and John's smile widened at the same time. Movement behind the sniper caught his attention. The spotter was back on his feet, struggling with the SMG.

The sniper drove a solid kick into John's chest in his momentary distraction. The force was enough to push him back, his foot kicking the sniper rifle behind him. The spotter fired, his weapon cradled with his left forearm, the hand still mangled and dripping blood. John dove and rolled, as the suppressed burst chewed into the wood. He grabbed the sniper rifle and swung the muzzle around, bracing the weapon against his body.

As the rifle came up, the sniper had his knife out and lunged at him. John squeezed the trigger, and the Barrett 82A1 erupted. The .50 BMG round blew a chuck out of the sniper's ribs, nearly tearing the man in half. But the bullet continued through the mercenary's body and exploded the spotter's head like a melon. The shot still echoed in the distance, but John reacted fast, pivoting and rolling to rest the rifle on the wooden deck. He looked through the scope, where the second sniper team watched the road below.

They heard the shot. John knew they did. There's no way anyone could have missed the—

"Falcon Two, this is Falcon One, what is your target?"

He saw the duo now, settling his crosshairs on the sniper. They were still looking down the clearing, thinking that's where this team would have been shooting.

"Falcon Two, I repeat—"

John shifted his aim, seeing the spotter turn to look directly at him through the scope. Before the man realized what was happening, John's rifle boomed again. The muzzle blast vibrated the air, the weapon's muzzle brake throwing out plumes of powdered snow to each side. The spotter fell back, his body obscured by the red mist.

The enemy sniper flinched in surprise but pivoted his own rifle to face John. Unexperienced on this weapon, John now found himself in a battle against a trained sniper, far more familiar with the process of putting rounds on target at long distances.

He had a little more time and was aiming at a standing target when he took the spotter out. The sniper presented a smaller, more dangerous problem. Still, John had the advantage, already being in position, while his opponent shifted around. Settling in to take his shot, he let out half a breath and tensed his finger. An eternity passed through his mind. When the trigger broke, the thunderclap and muzzle blast rendered his eyes and ears useless for a seemingly endless stretch of time. John wondered if the enemy had also sent over a bullet with his name on it.

John tightened his jaw and peered into the scope. His shot had torn a gouge through the top portion of the sniper's weapon, shearing the scope off, before passing through the man's upper torso. John took in a deep breath, and blew it out through his mouth, in a cloud of vapors.

John had hoped for the easy way in, but a trio of .50 caliber rounds ringing off the rock walls was quite an alert.

"The hard way, then."

***

The distant thunderclap drew Marvin's attention away from organizing the gear in the H1. He looked up through the trees, trying to spot the commotion in the distance. They had parked far away from the clearing to avoid the eyes of the spotters, but that put him well out of range of any optics that would allow him to see if John was ok. He shoved the rifle into the back and slammed the tailgate shut.

He stepped up into the driver's seat and turned the key, waking the mighty beast. Two more cracks split the air, only seconds apart. A high caliber rifle no doubt. The snipers. Marvin whipped the Hummer onto the road and sped toward the clearing. After a sharp left, the military vehicle clawed its way up the rough terrain, lurching and bouncing on its suspension as the three hundred horses under the hood ascended.

This was a stupid plan, and he knew it. Driving a large, loud utility vehicle right into the line of fire of two shooters, slinging heavy anti-material rounds down range was a sure way to get killed. Marvin's only hope was that the engine would bleed off enough energy to protect him inside if they started shooting at him. He spotted the first platform, along the southern ridge and veered in that direction, knowing that was John's chosen target.

With the rough bouncing, Marvin had a hard time identifying the man standing with a rifle cradled in the crook of an elbow. Van Pierce pulled the steering wheel hard, skidding to a stop and kicking up a spray of snow. He opened the door and stepped out, pressing his body against the fender, bracing his arms on the hood as he drew his pistol.

"Christ, is that you, John? I thought you were dead."

The Army Ranger strode down the steps along the back of the structure, resting the Barrett rifle against one of the supports. "Then why come up here? Sounds like a sure way to join me if I was dead."

"I didn't think it all the way through."

John turned his head, looking up toward the top of the mountain.

"What is it?" Marvin asked.

"Quiet," John said, holding a finger up as he turned his head slowly. "Do you hear that?"

Van Pierce stepped around to the back of the H1 cupping a hand behind his ear. There was a slight hum in the air. A high pitched whine that grew in volume and number. "The welcoming committee is on its way."

"We need to make a stand here before advancing," John said., reaching for the sniper rifle.

"No," Marvin said, pulling the tailgate open and retrieving his M16. "You need to suit up. I'll hold them off."

John nodded and put a hand on Marvin's shoulder. He reached into the Humvee and pulled a large plastic and steel case, letting it fall to the ground with a thud. He grabbed two more suitcase-sized boxes and set those on top. "You better get to work, then."

With a smile, Marvin shook his head, slid the barrel of his M203 forward and loaded a grenade. "I'll try to save some of the fun for you."

Van Pierce pulled the sling of the rifle over his body and started his trek up the hill. As the distant hum grew louder, he pressed his body against a tree and braced his weapon, aiming at the top of a ridge. A snowmobile crested the top, and he depressed the trigger of his M16, spitting out a three-round burst. Following with a second salvo, the bullets kicked up snow, but two rounds sparked against the approaching vehicle.

The driver swerved just as the man sitting behind him opened up with his submachine gun, sending the shots wide. Marvin blew out a breath and led his target, clicking the fire selector to semi-automatic. His next pair of rounds found their mark, punching holes into the driver's torso, sending the snowmobile careening.

The gunner on back rolled and came up into a crouch, but three quick trigger presses sent him to join his buddy. Marvin stepped out into the clearing and continued up the path. As more engines approached, he found a depression in the snow and dropped down, switching back to burst fire mode. Two more snowmobiles came into view in the distance. He fired three bursts, all missing but the return fire was equally ineffective as the drivers spoiled their gunners' aims maneuvering to present a harder target.

Switching his grip to the under barrel mounted M203, Marvin fired a 40mm grenade at the lead vehicle. With a *whump*, the projectile flew in a tight arc, and the snowmobile exploded into a ball of fire. The second pair of assaulters came straight at him, cutting the distance fast. The gunner fired a stream of bullets stitching up the snow. Van Pierce rolled to the side, drawing his Beretta. He fired five quick shots from the pistol, one-handed, cracking the windscreen and convincing the driver to rethink his strategy.

The snowmobile fishtailed to a stop, as the gunner leaped off the back and advanced with his HK UMP45 spitting lead. Marvin released the rifle and pressed the pistol between both hands, returning fire until the man dropped. He holstered his sidearm and grabbed the M16, ejecting the magazine. The driver was struggling to unsling his weapon at the same time. Marvin won the race, inserting a fresh mag and thumbing the bolt release, before punching several holes into his opponent with a trio of bursts.

He trudged up through the thick snow, sliding the barrel of his M203 forward and ejecting the spent shell. Taking cover behind the snowmobile, he reached for another grenade on his belt and fed it into the launcher's chamber, clicking it closed. Engines swarmed in the distance, as he swapped his partial magazines in his pistol and rifle for full ones.

The M203 thumped again, sending a 40mm high explosive grenade into the cluster of vehicles cresting the next hill. The blast flipped one of the snowmobiles on its side, and a second one rocked back like a bucking bronco. The blast and the shrapnel killed three of the men, but a fourth rose up from behind one of the trashed vehicles, firing his weapon.

Pain and fire lanced MVP's left forearm. The round passed through the flesh and muscle of his arm, before striking his vest. The shock from the wound and the bullet hitting his chest plate knocked him back. He rolled to one side and returned the favor, his M16 emitting a plume of fire and fury. The bursts cracked off chunks of fiberglass and punched holes into the mercenary's torso and arm.

Two more snowmobiles leaped over the hill and raced down, the gunners in back pinning Marvin behind his cover. He reloaded his rifle but had to leave the spent shell in his grenade launcher. In a crouch, leaning on the chewed up husk of a downed snowmobile, he put enough fire on his enemies to keep them back. The drivers swung the tails of their snowmobiles around, sliding to a stop as the gunners dismounted and approached, blasting away with their SMGs.

Marvin pressed his body as close to his cover as he could, blindly spraying bullets until the thunderous click of an empty chamber signaled the end of his defiance. Letting the M16 fall, he drew his sidearm and came up firing. The 9mm bullets peppered the area around the oncoming soldiers but did little to deter their assault. A bullet tore into his side as two more hammered his chest, the ballistic plate stopping the rounds from penetrating.

He fell onto his back, on top of his rifle, and the pistol slipped from his grasp. One of the soldier's circled around, ejecting an empty magazine and retrieving another. Marvin Van Pierce lay his head back, closing his eyes with a defiant smile. *Go ahead, you son of a —*

Mechanical thunder caused him to flinch. He felt no impact, but the machine continued to roar. It was a relentless pulsing of the air, each concussive blast reaching him only a split second apart from the last. The closest merc staggered away, a red mist in the air where he stood. A second man shouted and fired at someone behind Marvin. Another ear-splitting raucous sounded, and its raw power severed the solider's arm from his body in a ragged mess. The man's chest exploded open, and he collapsed in a heap on the red snow.

The snowmobile drivers were firing now, their HK UMPs letting out light staccato popping compared to the approaching beast. Marvin heard the whirring and clunking of an advancing machine just before it's explosive shouts of rage filled the air once more.

John stepped into view, donning a Juggernaut suit, it's power-assisted limbs humming and clicking with each step. He held an AA-12, fully automatic shotgun, with one arm, inserting another 32-round drum of 12 gauge shells into the weapon, while bullets pinged off his armored hide. His firearm reloaded, John cut the last two mercenaries down with two well-placed bursts of double-aught buckshot.

"You alright, Director?" His voice was amplified by the suit's audio system as he spoke.

"I will be," Marvin said, slamming his M203 shut, loaded with another HEDP round. "Now let's go crash this little shindig."

CHAPTER 34

"You good to go?" John asked.

Marvin secured the bandage on his arm, double checking the grazing wound across his rib. "I'm good."

John's world was encased in the power-assisted armored suit. The thick helmet cut off a good deal of his peripheral vision, and the oversized neck guard jutted out, obscuring his vision along the lower edge. The suit's aluminum oxynitride visor warped his view, but the curve was necessary to provide the bullet resistance at all angles of attack.

His breathing was incessant white noise in his ears, almost overpowering the digital sound amplification. Every step he took, he felt a soothing vibration, as the motors bore the brunt of the effort. Powered servos propelled the behemoth up the mountain, through the freshly fallen powder. The suit's mic picked up the distant roar of engines. Another wave of snowmobiles surged toward them.

He raised the AA-12, but Van Pierce beat him to the punch, greeting the attackers with a grenade that impacted directly with one of the vehicles. His M16 spat out a burst, but the reports sounded like a muffled drum beat after the Juggernaut's sound suppression clipped a few dozen decibels. John's shotgun, even firing automatic bursts of 12 gauge shells, barely bucked in his arms, the feedback dulled considerably by the powered joints.

The enemy halted their advance, the drivers opting not to charge headlong into a wall of buckshot, coming at them at three hundred rounds per minute. Making a stand above, the mercenaries utilized their high-ground advantage, presenting far more difficult targets. They fired down on the machine storming the castle.

Inside the suit, the bullets rattled the outer shell but failed to inflict any damage other than scuffing the outer layer. To John's ears, he was walking through a hailstorm, the impacts ringing hollow within the confines of the Juggernaut. His breathing increased, and he gritted his teeth, letting out a grunt as the shotgun fired again.

John dropped the empty ammo drum, the last of the 32-rounders, and reached across his left hip for one of the 10-round box mags. In the suit even a basic action required more concentration as the disconnect from flesh to weapon made the task difficult. He took his time as the enemy poured on the fire. A forceful thump rocked him to one side, and shrapnel sprayed the right side of his body.

The Juggernaut's composite armor absorbed the majority of the blast, but the concussive wave stole the air from his lungs. He sent the bolt home and brought his weapon up again taking aim at the wall of snowmobiles providing cover for the shooters. He selected the magazine loaded with solid slugs for this task, blasting away at the barrier with heavy one-ounce lead projectiles that punched huge holes into the thin skin of the recreational vehicles.

Another grenade arced through the air sinking into the snow nearby. The Juggernaut's power-assisted limbs propelled him to the side, far enough to minimize the blast. His shotgun roared, the last few slugs shredding the snowmobile and the man behind it.

"I'll break the line," John said, reloading again. "Get ready to move ahead."

"Just give me the signal," Van Pierce said, his digitized voice reaching John through the suit's speakers.

The motors revved, as John's armored form rushed headlong toward the enemy. The volume of fire increased, a static-like crackling shaking the air inside. Rounds landed flush against his limbs, the impacts registering as a dull ache through his joints. Covering the last ten meters, John emptied the magazine with two long bursts, the first shattering the already mangled husk of a snowmobile, the second tearing holes and severing limbs from two unfortunate mercs standing their ground.

The firing slowed as the soldiers scattered, only shooting occasionally while they fell back. Another grenade bounced off of John's shoulder, landing at his feet. He had barely enough time to bring his arms up and shield his face from the blast. Shrapnel washed over the suit embedding into his AA-12, rendering the weapon useless. He scanned the battlefield as one of the soldiers approached, weapon up and hammering away with well-placed rounds, hitting him around the visor.

"Did you just throw that grenade at me?" John asked. He hurled the damaged shotgun like a tomahawk, busting the man's face, splitting flesh and crushing bone.

An engine revved, and John turned on his heel, ready to face another wave of gunners. One of the mercenaries had jumped on the last functioning snowmobile, opened the throttle and flew at the Juggernaut. The driver leaped off, sliding and rolling across the packed snow as the vehicle careened ahead. John sank his stance low, bracing for the impact. The snowmobile collided with him head-on, but the Juggernaut's powered extremities stopped the five hundred pound machine. He slid back nearly a meter, the jarring blow reverberating through his body.

The mercenary got to his feet, drawing his pistol and firing at close range, hoping to hit something vital. John pressed inward as the exo-suit's hands dug into the fiberglass and steel. With a shout, he hoisted the vehicle over his head and brought it down on top the man, as if he were just an insect stinging him. Another soldier snuck up from behind, planting something on the suit's backpack. Twisting his waist, and pivoting around, John struck the man with a powerful backhand blow that crushed his jaw and cracked his vertebrae, sending his body hurtling five meters away in a flat spin.

A split-second later, the explosion from the grenade on John's back drove him forward and onto his knees. He struggled to his feet as the shooting started up again, the mercenaries finding their bravery once more. The suit's servos coughed and stuttered, the limbs almost seizing as he rose. Another grenade blast kicked up a plume of dirt, rocks, and snow, but that one landed near a cluster of mercenaries.

Marvin ran up to join John, sliding on his knees behind a destroyed snowmobile. He shouldered the M16 and fired a burst, hitting another soldier. This time the rifle's reports bled through the gaps and cracks in the Juggernaut suit.

John felt two sharp slaps on his back. "We can make it to Windham's house," Marvin said. "You march ahead, and I'll take care of the rest of these guys."

***

Pryce's fingers dug into the arms of his chair. He leaned forward watching the battle on the camera feed. Some idiot let Van Pierce escape, and now he was standing shoulder to shoulder with John Stone. A bead of sweat trickled down his temple as the first wave of mercenaries rushed down the mountain to meet them. His breath escaped him when John tore through a line of soldiers in one of his Juggernaut suits.

Balling up his fists, he pressed his knuckles against his head. "Mr. Gordon. Please tell me you've called the rest of the men back from the other patrols."

"Yes, I did, sir."

"I need them to circle around to the back and stop those men from getting in here."

"Of course," Gordon said. "Shall I join them?"

"No," Pryce's reply came out too fast. Too panicked. "I'll need you here just in case that maniac, Stone, makes it through."

His enforcer nodded, pulling the Glock 21 from his holster and checking the chamber for a .45 ACP round in the chamber before putting it back. He took his jacket off, hanging it on the hook of a coat rack near the door and started rolling up a sleeve as he left to relay Pryce's orders.

* * *

Sparks flew, as another burst struck the power pack of the Juggernaut. John struggled to move, the suit's left leg dragging. He could feel one of the elbows losing all power, as the limb weighed his arm down.

"My suit's losing power," he said.

Van Pierce crouched behind him, peering around his mobile cover and firing at a soldier, each trigger press sending a single supersonic 5.56mm round slicing through the cold air. Two of the bullets missed, but the third punctured the man's throat, severing his spine as it passed through, killing him instantly.

"One more push," Marvin said. "We just need to make it another ten meters."

The opposition had thinned considerably, but they could hear more men approaching in trucks and on foot. At the rear entrance of the large cabin, John punched a hand through the solid oak door and tore it free of the hinges. He pulled at the panels along the side to reveal the extraction handles.

"Give me a hand. This suit is toast."

Marvin kept the rifle in one hand and used the other to pull the uncovered red handles, popping the plates apart. John pushed free, separating the sections of the Juggernaut suit keeping him locked into the beast. He climbed out, and the freezing air hit his sweat-soaked body like a concussive force. His muscles tensed for a moment as his feet found the ground.

"I'm going after Pryce," John said, pulling the Colt 1911 from his drop leg holster.

"Go. I'll hold them off here," Marvin said, pulling two unused grenades off of the belt of a dead mercenary. "Can't let any of these goons get the drop on you from behind can we?"

CHAPTER 35

The warm air inside was a welcome change, but John knew he couldn't get complacent now. With his mind focused on finding and stopping Pryce Windham, the soreness and fatigue had long left his body, leaving him feeling a decade younger. He sliced around a corner, weapon up at a high compressed ready position, clearing the intersection at the home's back door.

Two men came down one of the halls, one talking rapidly, making his words difficult to make out. John stepped into a small room, keeping his body up against the wall as the approaching boot steps grew louder. He saw the muzzle of a rifle moving into view and brought his fist down hard against the man's forearm, cracking one of the small bones. The weapon swung down from his grasp, and the soldier's cries of pain were cut short when John's elbow smashed into his face, knocking his front teeth loose and wrecking his nose.

The second man whipped his rifle around, but John already pressed out with his pistol. Three rounds clustered tightly over the man's heart, and the man's body dropped limply to the floor. John would have preferred taking both men out quietly, but he figured Pryce knew he was already here, which would explain why those men were in such a hurry to get to the back exit.

The hall split into two directions, one turning where the two men came from, the other running the width of the cabin, past a series of knee-to-ceiling picture windows, before also cutting around the corner. Marvin's weapon started barking outside, the blasts muffled in the house. John would have to trust that no one would be able to get past MVP and sneak around from behind. He opted to head the direction from where the soldiers had come.

John's pace was quicker than normal, only giving the few rooms a casual sweep of his pistol, figuring most of the opposing force would already be outside dealing with their approach, judging by their sheer numbers. The hall opened up into a large living room with a massive fireplace in the center, the flames inside crackling.

He could see the other end of the room where the second hall also led to the living space. The chances that Pryce would have been hiding in one of the rooms on that end seemed unlikely. John advanced, positioning himself behind one of the many wooden support beams as he surveyed the area. The place was picturesque, massive bay windows opening up the mountain scenery around them. John focused his attention on the spiral staircase near where the other hall came to an end.

Taking a step out into the open something felt wrong, his instincts screaming at him. John pulled back behind the beam sinking into a more stable stance and taking another look at the area around the fireplace.

"Mr. Stone." The voice was cold, like a snake. "You certainly don't disappoint."

John snapped the front sight of his pistol at one of the tall-backed leather chairs facing the bay windows. A man stood up, tall and lithe. A hint of recognition clawed at the Ranger's mind. The man had his sleeves rolled up, his head shaved bald. He stepped around the chair and John saw the pistol tucked into a holster in his waistband, in front of his body.

"Mr. Stone. I've been expecting you."

It was then that John recognized the man. Mr. Gordon. Warren Ratcliffe's head of security. He appeared taller now, with more muscled packed onto his sprinter's frame.

"Thought you were dead," John said, holding his pistol at a low ready position. "I remember snapping you in half like a twig."

The enforcer smiled. "Things will be different this time."

"Yeah, because I'll make sure you stay dead."

John raised his pistol, but his opponent was a blur, sidestepping and drawing his own gun. Before John could get off a shot, Gordon already cleared his holster and fired.

* * *

The blast launched a mercenary into the air, his body shredded by the last of Marvin's grenades. Ice and debris rained down as the firing slowed. Van Pierce worked the charging handle of his M16 and brought it up, taking care to place his shots carefully, no longer using the weapon's burst fire mode. A trio of cracks found their marks on an advancing soldier.

Marvin whirled to his left as another group approached, trying to force him back or pin him down. He lowered his body, lying prone behind the Juggernaut suit that John had shed before going after Pryce. The enemy rounds thudded into the armor, and Marvin's M16 barked back, biting into the flesh of the man on the far end.

"John, I hope you find your man soon," he said, to no one in particular, readjusting his body. "I'm not sure how much longer I can hold these guys back."

A bullet hit nearby, spraying Marvin in the face and neck with dirt and snow. He answered back with three crisp presses of the trigger, making his attackers rethink their rush.

* * *

Gordon's 45 caliber rounds ripped splinters from the support beam. John spun around, leaning out from the other side to get a better angle on his fast-moving target. He fired several rounds, shattering one of the floor-to-ceiling windows. A gust of wind whipped through, sending a flurry of snow inside. John didn't let any of the chaos pull his attention away. It was just background noise to him.

The last time John faced this man, he was dangerous enough, armed with a 9mm Glock 19. He didn't want to believe this was the same man. This foe was faster than he remembered. More fearless. Bullets ate away at the wooden beam, flushing John out into the open. He stayed low and sprinted for another column. He heard the Glock 21 thundering, as the rounds punched into the luxury furnishings against the backdrop.

Just as John had hoped, his opponent expected him to stand and fight, so the quick movement worked in his favor this time as he dropped to a knee behind cover and fired until his slide locked. None of his shots hit Gordon, but it forced the man to move so that he could reload his 1911.

John heard the polymer mag from his opponent's weapon hit the floor, but before he could capitalize, Gordon had already thumbed the slide stop and his pistol was hammering away again. His Glock had a capacity of thirteen rounds, but John only had seven-round magazines for his 1911. He was face to face with a cold-blooded killer, using a handgun with greater capacity. John would be reloading twice as much if they kept up this pace.

As he moved forward to close the distance, John's pistol ran dry again just as he reached the fireplace in the center of the spacious room. He slapped in another mag and used the slingshot method to send the slide forward. Bullets chipped at the stone base, showering the area with sharp fragments. John felt a stinging pain across his upper arm. He leaned out and fired once, maneuvering to the other side.

Through the fireplace flames, he spotted Gordon rushing him. John propped his arms against the hearth and pressed the trigger, firing four rounds to deter his assailant. The 230-grain hollow point slugs tore into the burning logs, spitting sparks and fire through the fireplace, but it was too little, too late. Gordon returned the favor. John barely avoided the bullets and blaze of the embers spitting at him.

Throughout the entire fight, the enforcer had been relentless, constantly pressing the attack with a steady rhythm of rounds. And then the shooting stopped. Was this a trap? Did his opponent expect him to investigate? A thousand other thoughts sped through John's mind in that brief moment. He was already pivoting to get a better angle, pistol held steady when a flash of movement spoiled his aim.

The 1911 bucked twice, the slide locking to the rear. Gordon circled and stepped up onto the wide wrap-around hearth, launching himself up. His body was horizontal, and John's shots fell well-below his target. Gordon's body spun in a barrel roll, as his foot came slamming down on John's arms. A shockwave reverberated through his shoulders and neck, as his pistol clattered to the ground.

John swung a huge right hand, but Gordon shuffled back, letting the blow slip by. John reached out to grab his gun from the floor, but his savvy opponent flicked his foot out nonchalantly, sending it sliding across the floor. Gordon spread his arms out wide, flinging his empty Glock to the side.

"I guess we'll have to settle this up close and personal," John said.

"Maybe it's better that way." Gordon's smile was unsettling. "I may just stop at returning the favor and severing your spinal column." His smile faded. "Or perhaps I'll crush your skull."

CHAPTER 36

Ears ringing, his breath pulsing out in thick plumes, Marvin reached into his dump pouch for the last of his partially-spent magazines, and slammed it into his M16. He pressed the paddle to release the bolt and hurried to bring the sights back up. Three, four, five shots split the air as another mercenary fell and a second staggered back on his heels rolling behind cover again.

Pain suddenly lanced through his calf. Another bullet hit the ground nearby. Van Pierce fell to his side and rolled, in time to avoid the burst from a gunner that ran up on him from the right. His own rifle cracked twice, and he rolled again as the merc fell, sliding to a stop next to him. Coming up to a kneeling position, Marvin faced the front and fired at the man behind cover making a move.

Marvin's rifle clicked empty. His body moved on autopilot, sweeping his M16 away on its sling and drawing the M9 pistol in a fraction of a second. He fired his Beretta at the advancing soldier, who made it far enough to slide behind a rock. Marvin tried to move and get a better line of sight, but his leg buckled, sending a shooting pain up into his hip. He dropped to his knee again, and the mercenary tried to capitalize on his injury.

Marvin fell prone behind the Juggernaut and pulled the sling for his M16 free, tossing the empty weapon aside. Bullets thumped the ground, and the merc's SMG crackled. Marvin reached to the dead enemy at his side and grabbed his UMP45.

The muzzle flashes from both weapons filled his vision. The two exchanged fire while the mercenary advanced. Marvin felt something solid thumping into his chest, and he grunted as the air left his lungs. He gritted his teeth and fired again, this time the SMG found its target, bullets streaming until the magazine was empty. Marvin's hand went to his chest, resting on the ballistic plate as he fell back straining to suck in a breath of cold crisp air.

A voice in the back of his mind screamed at him. *Get up, Van Pierce!*

He pulled in a breath, got up to all fours, then pushed himself up onto his feet, leaning on the wall of Windham's cabin. He looked to one side, seeing all the small holes in the wood. Most of the rear facing windows had been shattered in the firefight. There was an eerie stillness in the air. No more shooting, the ringing in his ears receding.

That was the last of the mercenaries. Marvin had accomplished his task of keeping the enemy from coming up behind John. Now it was up to the Army Ranger to reach Pryce—

Distant gunshots, firecrackers in the distance, reached Marvin. He limped over to pick up his Beretta, placed it back into the holster, and grabbed a spare magazine from the dead mercenary for the acquired UMP. He tossed the empty one into the snow and reloaded the weapon, heading inside to help John.

* * *

The firefight had stopped, as Pryce watched Mr. Gordon disarm Stone. The elation he felt was palpable, sweet to his senses. Watching the fight on his security camera feeds didn't satiate his bloodlust, the urge to watch his head of security tear the head from John Stone's body overwhelmed him.

Pryce rose from his chair and hurried to the hall leading to the stairs. He stepped out of his office and heard the chaos of the fight before reaching the top of the staircase. Stopping at the rail, Pryce approached only far enough to get a good view but doing his best to stay out of sight. Mr. Gordon didn't need any distractions.

***

John's left fist dug into Gordon's body, impacting with a resounding thud. He followed with a right cross, landing flush on the jaw. Before he could press the advantage, his opponent turned with the punch, rotating around and driving his right foot into John's gut with a *whump*.

Staggering back, John's momentum stopped when his body hit one of the wooden support beams. He was able to sink and dip his head to one side as Gordon's foot lashed out, smashing into the hardwood surface. The thick oak beam, weakened by the firefight, cracked and toppled with a deafening crash.

John had difficulty controlling the range of the fight, being consistently forced on the defensive. He circled, stepping away as another flurry of kicks whipped by. John would have to bring the fight much closer, smother his opponent and dictate the pace of the battle. A sledgehammer roundhouse slammed into his thigh, sapping the strength from John's leg.

He stumbled as a spinning hook kick cracked into the side of his head.

John hit the ground, rolling once from the impact of the kick, his world still spinning. This was a much different foe than he faced in Ratcliffe's home. Stronger, faster, more fearless. More dangerous than he was prepared for. The man's movements felt artificial, his strength unlike anything John faced before.

Struggling to get back to his feet, John clenched his jaw, feeling a strange looseness just below his ear. A quick swipe of his tongue confirmed all is teeth were still in place, but the salty, coppery taste of blood filled his mouth. He spat out a red glob and brought his hands up. He expected Gordon to rush in quicker, but his opponent paced side to side, an arrogant smile spread across his face. He was a tiger toying with his prey.

"What are you waiting for?" John shouted.

Gordon shuffled in with a half step and faded back, nodding as he watched John's reaction. Again he probed, but John waited for the sudden movement, whipping a left hook, followed by a right uppercut. Both punches narrowly missed their targets.

A foot pounded into John's ribs, but his hand fell in time to entangle the leg, pulling his opponent into a tighter range where fists would be more effective than feet. Two jackhammer blows landed solidly against Gordon's face, the first breaking his nose, and the second slamming into his cheekbone.

John wrapped his hand behind the back of Gordon's head, letting go of his leg. He hit the enforcer with a short body blow and fired an uppercut right up the middle, hockey goon style. Teeth clacked together, and John felt Gordon's body slump downward as the man wrapped one hand on John's shoulder, and the other in the crook of his elbow.

John felt a foot trip his leg, and realized too late that Gordon was bringing the fight to the ground. The enforcer pulled John down and lifted his own legs up high as the two of them hit the ground. Gordon had John's arm trapped between his legs, driving his hips up to hyperextend his elbow in an armbar. John grabbed his trapped hand with his left and drove his weight forward, stacking his foe.

He pulled his hands closer to his body, pressing forward with his head, wedging the man's legs apart enough to prevent any damage to his elbow. With a quick bucking of his hips, Gordon shifted his legs just enough to trap John's head and one arm in a triangle choke.

The pressure grew as John felt something grinding in his jaw. Pain radiated out as his vision closed in, darkness swallowing the world around him. John used his free hand to grab a handful of his opponent's collar, and he hoisted Gordon into the air. Standing straight up, John held the man high above his shoulders, then dropped his weight forward. He heard a hiss and grunt over the *whump* of their bodies colliding with the hardwood flooring. He felt the pressure ease up, but his head and arm were still trapped. John repeated the process, but this time as soon as he drove his heels into the ground to stand, Gordon released the submission, letting John pull him up to his feet.

A knee thrust into John's midsection, sending a spray of spittle out. Gordon shoved John back just enough to steal his balance before hitting him in the chest with a front kick. Before his opponent continued the attack, John whipped out a series of hooks, finding only empty air. A roundhouse kick slammed into his inner thigh, and an elbow smashed into the bridge of his nose. John's world filled with stars.

Through blurred vision, he saw a shape close in fast. John dipped his chin at the last possible moment and thrust forward to meet his foe. Their bodies collided, John driving a shoulder into Gordon's gut.

The momentum carried them into a wooden beam, cracking it in half as they sprawled out, rolling along the floor.

John wiped his palms across his eyes, his vision finally starting to sharpen again. Fists and feet came at him in a flurry of violence, too fast for him to track and defend. Seemingly simultaneous impacts found his legs, arms, head, and ribs. Yet, even under the onslaught, John was able to lash out with a couple of strikes of his own.

Gordon's foot hit his chest, the shock of the blow rattling his teeth as his body crashed back against the side of a chair as it buckled and splintered under his weight. The enforcer stepped up onto another chair, launching himself up, his body turning through the air and coming down to drive his knee into John's head. He pulled his shoulder to one side as the blow crashed into the busted furniture.

John rolled into his foe, grabbing him with both hands and dragging him to the ground. Before Gordon could fight his way out, John landed a vicious elbow that bounced the man's head off the ground. John rose up to his knees to rain down punches with both hands. Pain shot up through his wrists and forearms with each blow, his fists landing on Gordon's head and arms.

He got his feet underneath himself again and pulled Gordon up. He hooked an arm under one of his opponent's, and grabbed a fistful of a pant leg, lifting his foe up and driving him down through an oak and glass table between the chairs.

Every breath of cold, thin, mountain air felt like it tore into the back of John's throat as he strained to pull in enough oxygen to stay conscious. His energy drained fast as his body struggled to keep enough adrenaline pumping to continue the fight. *Stay down,* he thought, looking at the enforcer.

Gordon's chest heaved, he too having difficulty keeping up this frenetic pace. Blood trickled out of the corner of his mouth, his swollen and battered face masked any discernible emotion. To John's dismay, the man got back to his feet, hands up, ready for the next round.

Neither man willing to concede, both combatants stepped forward. John guessed at his opponent's tactics, raising a foot just enough to check a leg kick and plowing ahead with jab and cross, letting his momentum carry him close. He wrapped Gordon in a bear hug, trapping his arms and squeezing. John felt one of the man's ribs pop and was rewarded with a grunt of pain.

Gordon drove a knee into John's inner thigh, making enough room between their bodies to snake a hand up, attempting to gouge a thumb into his eye. John twisted his head to one side, then thrust it forward. Their skulls cracking together as he released his grip.

John's foe caught him by surprise, recovering quickly from the headbutt, spinning as he lashed out with another hook kick. John leaned back just enough, to avoid the powerful blow. Gordon's foot touched down only long enough to rebound as his body turned back, slinging a roundhouse kick to the midsection. The foot buried deep into John's body, but he opted to absorb the blow. It was a sacrifice tactic, suffering the pain to entangle the leg.

With an arm draped around Gordon's kicking leg, John pulled him into a full-power overhand right. A heavy fist crashed into the man's jaw, and his opponent fell. John held onto Gordon's leg, torquing his body hard to one side, and dislocating the enforcer's knee.

The animalistic shout of pain and rage shook the walls as Gordon lashed out with his good leg to shove John back. Gordon rose to his feet, unsteady, the pain finally taking its toll. The Ranger advanced, intent on ending this once and for all.

Gordon never quit, still lashing out with quick strikes. John pushed through, letting the punches in so he could land his own thundering blows. Even with only one leg for support, the man was still dangerous, landing two strikes for every one of John's.

Blocking one of the incoming strikes, John lashed out and clamped a hand around Gordon's throat. He squeezed, feeling the man tense up to resist, but the soft tissue gave under the pressure. John blocked another blow with his left, but a second snuck through, the pain only serving to infuriate him. John stepped in close, bringing his elbow in close before extending upward, lifting Gordon up by his neck.

The man floated in the air unable to break the Ranger's iron grip. John stepped forward, and choke-slammed Mr. Gordon's body down onto the jagged wooden stump of the fallen support column. Vicious stalagmites of splintered wood pierced his body, perforating his vital organs before passing through the gaps in the front of his ribcage. Blood bubbled up from Gordon's lips as the last of the air escaped his punctured lungs. The fire and rage in his eyes faded as the life left his broken body.

CHAPTER
37

Mr. Gordon's howl reached straight into Pryce's core. The life drained from him as he watched Stone dislocate his man's knee. The urge to flee filled him, as his heart leaped up into his throat. He was halfway down the spiral staircase before he realized what he was doing. This man had tracked him halfway across the country with no resources.

He couldn't let John leave here alive. It would mean that he would be on the run for the rest of his life. Pryce reached the bottom step in time to watch in horror as John lifted Mr. Gordon up by the neck, and impale his body on the shattered remains of a wooden support beam.

Operating on a mix of fear and anger, Pryce circled around behind John, watching the man move. What he once thought was an invincible threat, a force of nature, now looked like a beaten man. Struggling to move as he lumbered toward something in the distance. With squinted eyes, Pryce spotted the pistol that Stone was going for.

He shouted and ran to close the distance as John reached down for the weapon. He turned his head just in time to see Pryce's foot catching him across the left side of his jaw. The kick landed flush, staggering the big man, dropping him to one knee.

Pryce sneered at the old, beat up, shell of a man. How could he have caused so much damage to his empire? He lashed out with a punch to John's face, and a big kick into his ribs.

"You think you can take me down?" Pryce's voice cracked. "Do you really think one man can bring my empire down?"

He grabbed a leg from the broken table and cracked it across John's back. Pryce kicked him hard in the stomach again, and John dropped to both hands and knees now.

Windham turned to retrieve the handgun on the ground, but something latched on to his dress shirt, pulling him back. The grip was weakened, and not like the beast that stormed his castle earlier. Pryce spun and smacked him away. He crouched in front of John, cupping his chin with a hand and lifting the man's head to meet his gaze.

"It's over. You're a dead man, Mr. Stone," Pryce said, a half-smile tugging at the right corner of his mouth.

Windham plucked a spare magazine from one of John's ammo pouches and turned to retrieve the Colt 1911, only a few feet away.

He picked it up and ejected the empty magazine. "Dead men tell no tales, and all that," he said with a chuckle. His laughter grew as he turned to face John again.

Pryce stepped away when he saw John back on his feet. His eyes wide, he struggled to slam the full magazine into the pistol. John closed the distance, as Pryce's shaking hands managed to reload the weapon.

The 1911 cracked and a .45 caliber slug struck John just under his collarbone. Pryce felt a machine-like hand latch onto his forearm, the pressure sending intense pain through his wrist and elbow. Pryce winced, gritting his teeth. He threw a punch with his free hand, the blow bouncing harmlessly off the side of John's face. Pryce followed with a second punch, praying for better results.

John caught his fist in the palm of his other hand. Slow, steady pressure building, the monstrous man squeezed both hands closed. Pryce's shouts grew in pitch, becoming wails and shrieks, as the knuckles in his left fist popped and fractured. Two deep cracks interrupted his pained screams as the bones in his right forearm cracked under the enormous pressure.

∗ ∗ ∗

Tears streamed down Pryce's face. Spit flew, as he shouted incoherent rants. John released his grasp, and Pryce collapsed to his knees. For weeks John had been pursuing this man. A shadow. An unknown and intangible threat. And now John looked down at a man with no more power over him.

A trail of saliva traced a line from Pryce's lip to his thigh, through gritted teeth. "This isn't over. I have powerful friends." He sucked in two hissing breaths.

John studied the pathetic facade of the man that ruined his life. His words had an element of truth. He had powerful and corrupt friends. Influence with enough people to shield him from the ramifications of his actions. Stealing the PEST device. The Guardian. Kidnapping his goddaughter, Emily. This was the man most directly responsible for the death of John's friend, Frank Colt. His brother-in-arms.

"I won't see a single day in a cell," Pryce said.

"You're right, Windham," John said.

"What?"

John wrapped his hands around Pryce's head, one at the back of his skull, the other over his jaw, lifting him to his feet.

"Dead men tell no tales."

"Wait, you can't—"

John snapped his neck, severing the spinal column with a wet crunch. Pryce Windham's lifeless body crumpled to the hardwood floor, eyes still wide open, fear, the last emotion he felt.

The world around John darkened, the sounds softening. Muffled footsteps approached, but he didn't have the strength to turn and face the whoever came up behind him. He saw justice through to the end for his friend, Frank. Now John was content with letting death claim him.

* * *

Van Pierce watched John wrench Pryce Windham's head a full 180 degrees, dumping his body in a heap at his feet. John's shoulder sagged. He took a step forward as his legs buckled.

Marvin ran over, dropping his SMG and draping one of John's arms over his shoulders, struggling to ease the big man down.

"It's over, John. We got him."

His eyes closed as his head rested on the hardwood floor. Marvin looked him over. His face was a battered mess, and he had no doubt that there had to be bruises and cuts all over his body to match. Just under his collarbone, Marvin saw a single bullet wound. There was a jagged exit wound on his back, that was still bleeding.

He put pressure on the wound, while he looked around the room for a phone, or any way to call for help. Marvin lowered his voice to keep John calm and relaxed.

"We got him."

CHAPTER 38

Light slipped in through half closed eyes. John blinked and turned his head, as the nurse opened the blinds.

"Good morning, Mr. Stone. And how are we doing?" he asked.

Even after a week in the hospital, John still felt a little worse every day. He was alive, but sometimes he wondered if survival was worth the recovery.

"Fine," he croaked through his teeth. His mandible had been fractured in the fight with Mr. Gordon and Pryce Windham, requiring his jaw be wired shut. It made speaking difficult and painful, but worse, it made eating solid foods impossible.

The nurse smiled as he wrote something down on a chart, fiddling with the array of beeping and whirring machines next to the bed. "Good. The doctor will be in to see you shortly." He placed the clipboard into a pouch next to the door on his way out.

John turned his head slowly, watching as two people stepped in, shortly after the nurse's departure.

"I still don't know how you survived all this," Parker said, glancing at John's chart.

Marvin Van Pierce followed in behind him, on a pair of crutches.

"Both hands broken, busted ribs, hairline fracture in your femur—"

"Parker, please," Marvin said. "He knows all of this already."

John used his elbows to pull himself up. Parker slid the chart back into the tray and moved to the side of his bed to help adjust it, letting him sit up.

"Take it easy, John. No need to get up on our account." Marvin eased himself into one of the chairs in the room.

"Curtis?" John asked through gritted teeth.

"Still in meetings," Marvin said. "He and Doctor Spencer are still presenting the rest of the information we recovered from Windham's home. There was a treasure trove of blackmail information, bank accounts, and other names."

John leaned back against his pillows, closing his eyes as he nodded. In the aftermath of the battle in the mountains, Van Pierce was able to convince local law enforcement for support until he could reach his government connections. With the Hostile Response Division compromised, he didn't know who he could trust.

Pryce Windham had influence over key officials, corruption snaking deep into the organization. After Miranda and Parker analyzed the information, she and Curtis traveled to Washington D.C. to present everything that was recovered, hoping to clear John of all accusations.

While his future was still a bit nebulous, the fate of the Hostile Response Division as an organization had already been decided. "What are you going to do now?" John asked, his words coming slowly.

Marvin rubbed at a small dent in one of the aluminum crutches. "With the HRD all but shut down, I was thinking about heading back out to Hollywood. Step behind the camera and do some directing this time." He looked up with a grin.

"Seriously?" Parker asked, pulling a file from his backpack.

"No, Mr. Lewis. I was just being facetious. The truth is, I'm not sure where my path goes from here, but I'll have to stick around to answer some questions, I'm sure."

John looked at the file in Parker's hand, nodding his head questioningly toward the pages.

"Oh, this?" Parker handed John the file as he sat in the other empty chair. "As you know, because you gave Curtis the name Windham, Miranda put together a little collection of info that Director Van Pierce used to help track him down. This is just the rest of the information that she wasn't able to secure earlier. The deep dive, if you will."

"What am I supposed to do with this?" John asked.

Parker shrugged. "Just some light reading."

"This is everything that is known about Pryce Windham," Marvin said. "A little something to provide closure, now that you've found the man responsible for killing Frank Colt."

John just stared at the plain beige file folder. "Thanks."

Marvin rose to his feet with a grunt. "Let's get out of here, Parker. John's got a tough day of rehab today."

Parker stood. "Thank you, John." He followed Marvin to the door before turning around. "For everything, I mean."

John nodded, a hint of a smile forming. He watched the two men leave and rubbed a thumb along one of the corners of the file. He tossed it onto the tray next to his bed and pressed his finger to the button on the side rail, lowering his head as he lay back.

For the past few months, John had been seeking justice. Warren Ratcliffe shook John's world apart. But he was just a lap dog for the puppet master, Pryce Windham. With both men dead, John finally had closure. Though he had been able to sleep through the night, it wasn't until now that he felt he could truly rest.

DID YOU LIKE THIS BOOK?

Let us know by leaving a review. It only takes a moment and helps us, and independent authors, tremendously.

In our schedule of books, we have a ton of different ideas we would like to work on, but if you loved reading about John Stone, and want us to continue to tell his story, you, as the reader, can let us know directly. It is very difficult for us to get an idea of which books work without that feedback.

Let others know about it as well, and encourage them to leave a review. Right now, our future releases are all based on reader feedback, so if we don't know you liked the book, future sequels will sit in the queue along with the rest.

Thank you in advance!
The Manning Brothers

Want more from the Manning Brothers?
Here's a sneak peek of Execution Style
A Nine Millie Espionage Thriller

CHAPTER 1

Miami. The city was blessed with beautiful weather and filled with beautiful people all year round. The party scene was a haven for the rich, and Jordan Blaise was rich. New money, a millionaire who came upon his fortunes within the past few years. It was this wealth that afforded him the clothes, jewelry, and cars that helped him fit in with the crowd. The attention he got as a wealthy young man in Miami was a vast improvement over his paycheck to paycheck days as a wage slave.

Saving up for a car during the market crash of 2008, Jordan found himself in the perfect position to use that nest egg to take advantage of the recovery, entering the market at its lowest point in over a decade. He saw his investments climb before discovering the rush of day trading. Jordan spent the next few years clawing his way to financial freedom, finally earning the lifestyle he once envied while working a day job.

Now he sat behind the wheel of a Lamborghini, with two beautiful women riding with him. The blonde in the passenger side had her head and one arm out the window, laughing and shouting at the suckers they passed. A raven-haired woman with emerald green eyes sat in his lap with one arm wrapped around the back of his neck, and the other steering the powerful sports car as they sped down Florida's famous A1A. Her floral perfume filled his nostrils as he breathed in deeply.

Jordan kept his foot on the gas and wrapped his hands around the woman's slim waist as he let out a loud victory howl, feeling the wind whipping through his hair.

"My life is in your hands," he said, closing his eyes.

The trio of daredevils flew down the highway, shouting in glee as the fast paced thumping beats blared from the speakers.

Finally, he grabbed the wheel and took a series of turns, until they reached his rented beach house. He pulled the car up front and killed the engine, still laughing and cheering with his two dates. The night air cooled, but still held on to the humidity. A thin sheen of perspiration covered his body, from the thrill of their ride.

The trio staggered into the foyer of the large house, and Jordan struggled to find the lights. When he finally hit the switch, the warm incandescent glow highlighted the marble floors and designer furniture in the living room.

"Ladies, make yourself at home. I'll get us some cocktails."

Jordan made his way to the kitchen and pulled a bottle of champagne from the refrigerator. He searched the cupboards, looking for suitable glasses, giving up and picking three mismatched tumblers. Pinching the glasses between the fingers of one hand, he snatched the neck of the bottle with the other and headed back into the living room.

The women were in the guest bathroom, giggling and talking in low voices. With a goofy grin, Jordan placed the drinks on the coffee table and headed over to the stereo. He docked his phone in the charging station, picking up the playlist where they left off in the car.

Jordan pulled a small bag of white powder from his pocket and dropped it next to the glasses. He unbuttoned his shirt and took off his belt, dropping onto the plush sofa, sinking into the soft cushions.

The door behind him opened, and one of the women walked over. He kept his eyes shut, listening to her stiletto heels clicking on the floor as she sauntered to him. The long strides told him it was the taller of the two, with the long raven locks falling in loose curls around her shoulders.

She slid her hands down his chest, settling on her knees, behind the couch as she nibbled on his ear.

"Where's your friend?" Jordan asked. "I've got some party favors here." He gestured to the cocaine and champagne on the table.

The woman leaned in close, letting her hair drape over his shoulder. "She'll be right out. I let her know I would help warm you up." She bit his earlobe and pulled away, plucking the soft flesh.

Again, the floral scent filled his senses. "What's that perfume you're wearing?"

"It's Jasmine." She snaked her hand into his t-shirt and gently raked her fingernails across the thin curly hair on the milky flesh of his chest.

"It's," he searched for the best word to describe the pleasant smell, "downright intoxicating."

"Well, we need to make sure your senses are nice and sharp for this." She reached behind her back and pulled the drawstring from her bikini top and pulled it over her head, letting the turquoise and white garment hang in front of Jordan's face.

He felt the woman's bare breasts pressing into the back of his neck as she laid her top loosely across his chest, like a necklace. He spread his arms out along the back of the couch, pressing his head back into her chest.

"I'm ready when you are," he said, barely containing his glee.

He felt her breath on his cheek as she leaned in.

She whispered into his ear, "You got too greedy, Blaise. Rebecca Flair sends her regards."

"Wha—"

She pulled the bikini top, wrapping the ends around each hand. It slid up his chest, wrapping it around his neck. Pulling the ends together, the woman turned to place her back against the couch and leaned forward, with the drawstrings draped over her shoulder.

Jordan gasped, struggling to slip a finger underneath the ligature to relieve some of the pressure. A thin piano wire embedded into the fabric sliced through the first few layers of his flesh as blood trickled down, forming a spreading crimson stain on the collar of the millionaire's two-hundred dollar t-shirt. In the throes of death, he kicked off of the coffee table, forcing his body up and over the back of the couch. The assassin rose to her feet, supporting the weight of his upper body by the garrote around his throat.

After a few more futile moments, his body went limp, as a gurgling raspy breath escaped his swollen parted lips. The mystery woman released her grip letting Jordan's body hit the floor. She turned to face him, tilting her head to make sure her target was dead. Satisfied with the outcome, she walked over to the beach bag on the other end of the room and pulled off her wig, revealing short cropped oak brown hair.

She dropped the wig into the bag and pulled out a short blue dress, slipping it over her head to cover her half-naked body. The woman straightened and smoothed the fabric and ran her fingers through her hair, checking the mirror to give it some semblance of style quickly. She blew a kiss at her reflection and scooped the bag up and pulled out her phone.

The woman took two pictures of Jordan's body, making sure his face was in focus and framed in the shot. On her way out, she grabbed the keys to the Lamborghini and left through the front door.

CHAPTER 2

Plano, Texas. The droning buzz of insects filled the warm humid air. A young woman stood in the center of an abandoned house, broken bits of plaster, trash, and other detritus covered the floors. Her breathing had only now slowed to a reasonable level as the adrenaline left her system. Her arms and hands ached, and the strength in her legs waned.

Massaging her wrist, the young woman looked at the scrapes and marks on her once terra-cotta skin. Years of staying indoors faded the color, but the intense training toughened her flesh, along with the muscle and bone underneath. Her name was Millie. At least the only name she remembered.

At her feet was a body. Eyes still open, the woman on the floor was covered in her own blood and lay in a large pool of the sticky red fluid. She tried to kill Millie, tracking her down to this small abandoned house to strike. Or more accurately, Millie had led the woman to the house to spring her trap. She spotted her assailant on her tail earlier that afternoon and had hoped to escape without having to engage.

Millie's training gave her the skills to detect the woman stalking her through the small Texas town hours earlier. Unable to break free to disappear, she knew it was only a matter of time before the hunter found an opportunity to take her shot. Millie had to take control of the situation, so she found a run-down neighborhood with a few foreclosed houses in disrepair. Millie made a show of digging around the house, to pull up some grass suitable for use as makeshift bedding, before heading inside.

The fight was over in a flash but had taken its toll on her. She disarmed her attacker the moment the other woman entered the house, forcing her to fight hand to hand. Millie banked on the fact that her pursuer focused more on firearms, and less on the up close dirty work that she had been taught.

The dead woman lay in the middle of the run down house, blood no longer pouring from the puncture wounds in the side of her neck. Millie still held the galvanized nail she used to deliver the killing blows. She let the sharpened bit of metal fall to the ground, settling into the layer of garbage. The woman carried a Walther P99 pistol, which she never had a chance to employ in the fight. Her keyring had only a single key fob with a Mercedes Benz logo, and a small USB flash drive. Millie couldn't find any identification or any other weapons. She shed her now blood-stained t-shirt and used it to wipe her hands clean, as best she could. She managed to keep most of the blood off of the tank top she wore underneath.

Pushing herself back to her feet with shaky arms, Millie ran her fingers through short, sweat-soaked hair and pocketed the keyring. She walked over to the pistol and press-checked it, finding a live round in the chamber. A breeze pulled the smell of the grass and bushes into the house, mixing with the salty tang of blood and sweat. The scents pulled Millie's thoughts into her past.

She pushed the memories to the back of her mind, heading outside to find the would-be assassin's car. The sun dipped below the horizon, painting the sky in oranges and reds. She could feel the temperature of the air dropping, but in the Texas weather, she knew it would hold on to much of the heat throughout the night.

Inside the Mercedes, the other woman kept a messenger bag in the back seat. Millie retrieved it and shut the door before slipping into the driver's seat. She placed the pistol into the center console and dug through the bag. *Jackpot.* Millie pulled out a fat roll of cash, mostly twenty dollar bills, but more than a few *Ben Franklins* hung out in the roll as well. She dug deeper into the bag and found a burner cell phone and a file folder with a few hard copies of what looked like pages about Millie's training and possible whereabouts.

They found her. They were hunting her now.

CHAPTER 3

Nine Years Ago

A nine-year-old girl, paralyzed by fear, sat on her knees in the middle of a dusty road. Her face was streaked with the tears that cut through the layers of dirt on her cheeks. She didn't remember when, or why, but she stopped crying what seemed like a lifetime ago. The young girl twisted her head slowly from one end of the street to the other. The sounds of gunfire and screams from the people in her village barely registered, only muffled shadows of what they were moments before.

Half an hour earlier, a fleet of pickup trucks rolled into the town, full of men armed with assault rifles, pistols, and shotguns. Without provocation, the army of marauders kicked down every door, pulling out anyone inside, before looting the houses, shops, and the church. The *soldiers* started burning the ransacked husks and rounded up the people, separating the children from the others. Without hesitation, the attackers gunned down anyone that put up a fight.

The little girl sat in the middle of the street, watching it all play out around her. She hadn't been making any noise, sitting still while they moved from building to building. She saw them load the kids into the backs of trucks, driving away one by one as each reached capacity. They pulled adults from the second group, looking for the weakest of the village. Lined up in front of their own burning houses, they were executed by firing squads. Were they the lucky ones?

"Hey, there's one more," one of the armed men said, speaking Spanish.

"How did you idiots miss her?" another asked.

He slung his AK-47 over his shoulder and walked over to the girl on the road. A few of the men in the crowd stepped forward to beg and protest. Each one fell as the soldiers struck them with their rifle butts. The man in charge of the marauders shouted over his shoulder for the others to maintain order, as he hooked a hand under the girl's arm, hoisting her up with an almost angry jerk. He shoved her forward as one of the villagers that had been struck stood up again.

"Kill them all. None of them would last a day in the camps," The lead soldier said. He grabbed a handful of the girl's long black hair and shoved her to one of the remaining pickups.

She flinched as the ear-piercing crackle of automatic gunfire split the air. The man opened the passenger door of the truck's cab and tossed her into the seat, shoving her into the middle as he climbed in. The driver got in on the other side and started the engine.

They discussed the best place to take their captive, with one suggesting that the rest of the trucks were only a few minutes ahead. They would be able to catch up quickly.

"I don't want to babysit this brat for six hours," the passenger said. *"Turn left up there. We'll take her to Sofia."*

***

The pickup bounced and rumbled over the rough roads for almost an hour. The man in charge had directed the driver to pull off the main road a while back. The truck's occupant's had been tossed about until they reached a clearing. The ride smoothed out, and a path led up to a ranch off in the distance.

"Pull over. Outside the gates. Don't go inside," the man in the passenger seat said, directing the driver to park the truck.

He pulled the girl out of the cab and shoved her forward. She almost fell to her knees, staggering ahead. She saw a woman approaching but quickly dipped her eyes back down watching the ground at her feet as the man prodded her ahead.

"We've got another one for you, Sofia," the man said.

"This is not what we agreed upon," Sofia said, speaking heavily accented English.

"You said girls. Five hundred each," he replied in broken English.

The girl didn't understand the exchange, keeping her eyes averted.

The woman bent down and pulled the scared child's gaze up with a finger under her chin. Sofia dressed like a school teacher, wearing a white button up shirt tucked into an ankle length dark blue skirt. Her eyes softened when she saw how scared the girl was. She gestured to another woman, also dressed as a teacher. *"Wait over there, please."*

The scared little girl nodded and shuffled her feet. The second teacher met her halfway, before leading her back into the safety of the compound's wooden post fence. The first woman turned to address the two men.

The driver held his rifle by its sling over his shoulder, letting his eyes wander everywhere but on the woman talking to his boss. The man in charge had his weapon hanging across his chest, hand resting on the grip, with the other placed on top of the rifle's fore end. Their discussion was terse, as they spat back and forth in short angry sentences, switching between Spanish and English.

Sofía pointed back to the truck and waved the two men away. The leader of the kidnappers adjusted his grip, holding his AK in a low ready position. He took a step forward, posturing as he spoke, nodding his head toward the little girl. The muzzle of his weapon rose, and the girl had difficulty following what happened.

Sofía brushed the rifle muzzle toward the ground, while her other hand flashed to her waistband. She circled her hand to the front, against her hip, and dropped her elbow, sending two sharp cracks. Two red spots puffed out from the man's shirt, and the sudden chaos sent the girl scurrying behind the other woman for protection.

With practiced ease, Sofía brought her hands together, gripping her pistol in both hands. The weapon spit out a spark, followed by a third thunderclap, as a hole appeared in the man's forehead.

In less than a second, she shot him three times. He was dead before his body hit the dirt. The second man looked on in wide-eyed horror. Every possible option he should take raced through his mind. He kept his weapon slung and turned to run for the truck. Sofía followed with measured steps, never breaking her stride as she put three rounds into the fleeing kidnapper between his shoulder blades.

She covered the rest of the distance and shot him in the back of the head. Sofía turned and walked back toward the girl, pulling a spare magazine from behind her other hip. She released the empty magazine, pinching it between her pinky and ring finger, before reloading her Officer's model 1911.

She spoke to the other woman and pointed to the two dead men. The second woman ran off to bring a group to clean up the mess. Sofía knelt in front of the girl and tilted her head to look her in the eye, again softening her expression to ease the tension. She spoke to the girl in Spanish, asking what her name is, saying that her's is Sofía.

"¿Cómo te llamas? Yo me llamo Sofía."

The child looked up at her perceived rescuer, and a fresh stream of tears began to flow from her eyes. She shook her head, either unwilling or unable to speak, much less give her name. In the trauma caused by the attack on the village, she could only recall the horrific scene of the grown-ups in her town viciously gunned down, playing on a loop through her mind.

"I had an aunt named Millicent," Sofia said. "You remind me of her. She was my favorite aunt, but I always thought her name was a bit too long for my tastes. Can I call you Millie?"

Want to continue the story?
Execution Style is available now at Amazon

More from The Manning Brothers:

Nine Millie: Execution Style
Chance Hunter: Hunter Killer
Ty Octane: Terminal Velocity
Miami Winter: A Scott Maverick Thriller

Also Available from the Manning Brothers
Superhero action and adventure!
Two Percent Power: Delivering Justice
Spilled Milk: Two Percent Power Book 2

Thank you for reading!

If you liked this story, and would like to find out about more, join the Manning Brothers reader group and stay up to date on the progress of ALL of our future books. You will receive a link to download FREE stories, as well as notifications keeping you up to date on all new releases. You'll also receive special offers, intended only for subscribers.

www.EvilTwinBrian.com/join

Made in the USA
Monee, IL
14 October 2020